SCRAMBLED

Cardiff Libraries
www.cardiff.gov.uk/libraries

Llyfrgelloedd Caerdydd
www.caerdydd.gov.uk/llyfrgelloedd

I Hel a'r plantos

SCRAMBLED

HUW DAVIES

Firefly

First published in 2016
by Firefly Press
25 Gabalfa Road, Llandaff North, Cardiff, CF14 2JJ
www.fireflypress.co.uk

A CIP catalogue record of this book is available from the British Library.

ISBN 9781910080368
ebook ISBN 9781910080375

This book has been published with the support of the Welsh Books Council.

Typeset by Mad Apple Designs

Printed and bound by: PULSIO SARL

1

It was the first day back after the summer holidays in Maesunig Comprehensive. The entire school was sat in the hall, waiting for the new headteacher. Nobody knew what to expect. There were rumours that he was a six-foot-eight monster, there were rumours he was a nasty four-foot-two hobbit. There were some who said she was a woman with yellow teeth and a stick, there were some who said he was an old man with a dog (and it was the dog who made all the decisions). What most people wanted was someone who would turn the school around and get it back on its feet, what with the old Head Mr Wiggins going a bit wonky at the end of last term.

Over the summer pupils' imaginations had created their own personalised headteachers, with steam coming out of their ears or battery acid spitting from their mouths when they shouted. Davidde hoped it would be someone who would let him get on with his drawing and reading; someone who would stop Lyndon Lyons and his gang from breaking his pencils and drawing phallic symbols in his school books. Davidde Nippers felt like he was the only one in the hall who wanted this newcomer to breathe fire, because realistically, he thought, things couldn't get any worse than they were already. If everyone else felt a bit intimidated and scared most of the time, they'd be in the same boat as him. It would be nice to have some company.

Davidde sat there and waited. There was a buzz in the hall, all eyes excited, and behind the eyes a sense of fear. Teachers hushed the students who were still speaking, though they looked nervous as well.

Then he strode onto the stage.

He had a suit on, with a waistcoat and tie. The tie didn't have any food on it, so he immediately had one up on Wiggy. He got to the lectern, put his hand on it, and surveyed the school with his other hand held behind his back. He held this pose for a minute. He took his time. Davidde's hopes rose. This was someone who wouldn't take any messing. The tension became unbearable.

And then he spoke.

'Hi, guys,' he said. 'It's lovely to be here!'

Davidde put his head in his hands. He could feel Lyndon Lyons and his gang relax immediately, and could almost hear them thinking, 'We'll have a right laugh with this one.' Davidde had hoped that his two GCSE years at school would pass quickly enough, but now they seemed like a life sentence.

The headteacher continued.

'It's a new start, folks, a fresh beginning for you and more importantly for me as well.'

He paused.

'Please allow me to introduce myself. The name's Evans. Mostyn Evans. Mostyn Bumford Evans. You can call me Sir, or Headmaster, but I don't really do formal myself – I'd prefer it if you called me Mostyn, or Moz, or even Evsie – though I'd prefer it if you didn't called me Bummers like some of them did at my last place – and that was just the staff!'

The headmaster stopped to allow people to laugh. There was silence.

'Tough crowd,' he said. 'Anyway, I want you all to forget what's happened before, let's start again. I've made a point of not finding out who the naughty ones are here, because no one's a naughty one to me until they've done something naughty. And even then they're not naughty, they are just someone who's done something a bit naughty. Can you see what I mean, guys?'

Davidde could see exactly what it meant. It meant the time Lyndon had set fire to his trainers didn't matter. It meant the time Dwayne Tight had spat in his cheese roll didn't matter. It meant the slate had just been wiped clean, ready to be filled up again, with Dwayne Tight's spit.

'As I drove up this morning,' continued the Head, 'I remembered little Blodwen Sykes. She wasn't the brightest tool in the box, if you see what I mean. In fact, she was what we used to call dull. Not very bright. And she'd admit that herself. But what she lacked in mental agility, she more than made up for with heart.

'Now Blodwen loved her dog, Smwt. She and Smwt spent a lot of time together, probably because they had a lot in common. I'm not saying Blod had a wet nose, pointy ears and a floppy

4

tongue,' he said as he did an impression of a dog, using his hands for ears and letting his fat tongue hang out of his mouth while he panted like a spaniel. He did this for a full minute. Some of the younger students laughed, everyone else, especially the staff, looked on in astonishment.

'No, the things they had in common were that they both had huge hearts, and that the dog was also a bit dull. Dogs are known for making the right choices by instinct, for being in exactly the right place at the right time. But not Smwt. What he was doing on that spit of sand with the sea coming in so quickly, no one will ever know. I'll tell you what we do know. We know that Blodwen wasn't going to see him suffer by himself. She was going to get to him and wait by his side until they were rescued.'

He paused and looked up at the ceiling, picturing Smwt and his brave owner together as the waves surged in.

'That's what I want from us all. I want us all to be like Blodwen and Smwt. Helping each other out, sensing the danger, stepping in when one of us is up against it. It could be your friend that you help, it could be someone you don't know, it could be someone you don't even like. It could be me, Mr Mantovani or Mrs Flegg. All I want to know is that we all do our best for each other. I know that I will do my best for you!'

He clenched his fists and screwed his eyes shut. It looked like he was going to cry.

'I know what you're all wondering, oh yes. What became of Blodwen and Smwt? How did they get out of that? Well, to cut a long story short, they didn't. The emergency services couldn't get close to them and they died, but the important thing is they died together, which I'm sure you'll agree is a much better thing than dying alone, especially in such horrific circumstances: the long, drawn-out, agonising process of drowning in the open sea. Thank you. Now let's lead out from the back with the older students...'

Art was first with Miss Pughes-Pervis. As usual she was dressed in black. She was excited about the new term and was waving her arms around like a great gothic windmill. The class waited for her to start. Dwayne Tight had found some clay and was making a demented hedgehog out of it.

The art room was a large rectangular space

with light coming in through the many windows that ran along one of the long walls. The large worktables had been painted black, because Miss Pughes-Pervis said that this allowed the students to work without any colour distractions. The walls had been painted black for the same reason. The floor was also black, because this made the room seem deeper, and the ceiling was black because it made it seem higher. The door was black, the chairs were black, and the shelves were black. Pencil sharpeners were black, pens were black and rubbers were black. Boxes of paints were black. There had been a campaign to have a whiteboard fitted in the room, but this was resisted because it wasn't black. It was the last place in the school that had a blackboard, but any chalk that was used was housed in a special holder that was, obviously, black. Miss Pughes-Pervis had tried hard to source black clay, but this had proved impossible. Dwayne's bright orange hedgehog stood out dramatically.

Miss Pughes-Pervis was now very still with her hands behind her back.

'Welcome back. And thank you for choosing Art.'

She looked at the ceiling and collected her thoughts.

'As I'm sure you know, we live in a violent world, but Art is the thing that can lift us out of it. There's no need to insult someone when you can draw a picture of them and take your anger out that way. There's no need to punch someone when you can make a sculpture and express your emotions safely. There's no need to stab someone when…'

'You can ram some paintbrushes up their nose!' shouted Dwayne.

Davidde hated Dwayne. He couldn't believe he'd taken Art. He'd probably want to make compositions out of his own snot and blood. In fact Davidde figured that Dwayne would probably prefer using Davidde's snot and blood, or even Davidde's internal organs if he could.

'Dwayne. I'm so pleased you've chosen Art. You've got a lot of anger to channel.'

'Aye, Miss. Watch this now!' He proved her point by biting the head off his hedgehog, flicking his own head and letting go so the wet orange hedgehog head landed on Ceri Barlow's new white shirt. (Her name was Ceri Barlow, but due to the fuss she made about the most trivial things she was universally known as Ceri Fuss by staff and pupils.)

'You're disgusting!' she shouted and ran out to get the clay off her shirt.

'Dwayne, love, it was great when you made the sculpture, but it wasn't so great when you spat it over Ceri. I'd like you to apologise while I speak to Davidde and Kaitlinn.'

Kaitlinn Trunk was the only person who did better than Davidde in their year in school. In some ways, they had a lot in common. They had both been brought up mostly by one parent, they were both usually the best in the class, and they'd both been given first names with eccentric spellings. Teachers had been stunned when the pair would spell onomatopoeia and diarrhoea faultlessly, when the parents clearly had more of a scattergun approach to spelling their children's names. Maybe it was this that drove them on to do so well at school. Maybe. But the fact remained that they saw each other as rivals, and it was a battle that Kaitlinn would win; though in Art Davidde ran her very close. There were things Davidde could do with a pencil that Kaitlinn couldn't dream of doing. One day Miss Pughes-

Pervis had run over a badger and killed it (she seemed to run over lots of animals when she was driving to school), and she went back for it to use as a still life exercise in class that day. She placed it artistically on a tablecloth and asked the class to look for the beauty in front of them. Somehow Davidde found it. He seemed to have a knack for drawing fresh roadkill that Kaitlinn couldn't match.

'I'm sooo delighted you've both taken Art. Art is the greatest thing. Good people take Art.'

'Miss,' Kaitlinn interrupted. 'What about Hitler?'

Davidde tried not to roll his eyes. She was such a know-all.

'What about him, Kaitlinn?'

'Well, he was good at Art, Miss, I saw it on the telly, but he did a few bad things didn't he?'

Miss Pughes-Pervis thought about this for a second.

'Yes, I suppose he must have taken Art at some point in his education, that is correct.' She frowned at the thought of someone being able to paint a decent picture and also being responsible for so much evil.

'He did take Art, Kaitlinn, but he never took Art with me!

'Now then you two, I've got some news. Seeing that you've both got so much talent, I've decided to try something different with you this year. It's something I've never tried before, so you're going to have to help me. I've decided that I want you to do the course in one year instead of two, because I don't want you getting bored with the subject. There are three projects for you to do, and the first one needs to be completed before half-term in October. There will be a moderator coming in to look at your work, so it's really important that it's ready.'

'But what will we do in the second year, Miss?' demanded Kaitlinn.

'We can do more advanced things – bolder ideas, bigger pictures, better roadkill!' She seemed genuinely excited and left them to think about it, while she helped Dwayne get the clay out of his hair that Ceri Fuss had just put there.

'Sounds like we're being put under a bit of pressure,' Davidde said.

'Pressure? Pressure? You don't know the first thing about pressure. Try being a woman on your own in this valley like my mum. That's pressure.'

'I was only saying,' said Davidde.

'Don't. You're making yourself look pathetic. Pressure. I can cope with a little bit of pressure,' she said. 'I cope with it every day.' She looked down her nose at him and then flounced off like an angry, red-haired horse.

2

That lunchtime, as usual, Davidde went to the library. Sometimes he talked to the librarian, Mrs Tubbins, an older lady with an elaborate grey beehive hairdo. He'd heard that at weekends she went out on a motorbike. He often wondered how she got her hair inside the helmet, or if she'd had one specially made to house her massively elongated head. She'd let him into the library but had left to make a phonecall.

He hadn't seen the astronomy books for six weeks. He'd read them all cover to cover a hundred times and it was like meeting up with old friends. He still liked to flick through and look at the pictures of the planets and their moons, and the photos of distant stars and galaxies. He found the exotic colours and shapes on the shiny paper relaxing, a reminder that there was something beyond this town, beyond this planet even. Even the smell of the books was comforting. He was alone and safe. He heard the door open on the other side of the room. He went back to reading about the Crab Nebula.

Then his head was six inches in front of where it should have been, and he felt pain at the back of his head. He turned around to see Dwayne Tight grinning wildly, screeching, 'BOOK FIGHT! BOOK FIGHT!' at the top of his voice. Davidde realised he'd been hit by a book thrown by Dwayne. The rest of Lyndon Lyons' gang piled into the room and ran around pulling armfuls of books off the shelves. They all wore identical expensive hooded jackets and gold chains. They split into two groups either side of the library and hurled books at each other, ducking behind tables and knocking over chairs to create better barricades. Lyndon Lyons threw *A History of Modern France* at Craig Smurfit and it caught him right in the face. He retaliated with *Desmond's Big Day*, which disintegrated as it left his hand, creating a smokescreen of pages. Dwayne realised that paperback books weren't any good and crawled away looking for *The Guinness Book of Records*. The battle continued; non-fiction definitely having the edge over children's literature. Davidde couldn't get out and was scared of getting hurt or in trouble. He also felt bad for Mrs Tubbins; there was no way he could stop all this, and she would be upset. She appeared at the door, surveyed the devastation and scurried off for back-up.

Books continued to shoot through the air, and the boys shouted and swore at each other. As the action peaked, Dwayne knew what to do. He had located a copy of Proust's *A La Recherche du Temps Perdu*, and it was just the job. Big, fat and heavy. He launched it with all his might.

Just before this, Mrs Tubbins' back-up had arrived in the shape of the new headmaster. He strode manfully into the centre of the library and stood still, with his hands on his hips. The boys stopped. The boys knew they were for it as they looked at the pages and the books on the floor, the waste, the intellectual carnage they had created.

And that was without the book Dwayne had just thrown.

Davidde saw everything from where he sat. He saw the Head walk in and pause, he saw Dwayne launch the book. It arced through the room, binder first, a perfect shot. The Head raised his hand and pointed seriously, and opened his mouth to speak. He got as far as 'Guys…' when the book caught him square on the temple. He went straight over and disappeared under the tables. There was complete silence.

Mostyn Evans reappeared a few seconds later rubbing his head. The Lyons gang looked worried.

'Listen, guys, I'm not going to start shouting,' he said.

Lyndon and his crowd looked down when he looked at each of them, trying not to laugh. Anything was possible now.

'The thing is, guys, I know you're in high spirits on the first day back, and a certain amount of horseplay is to be expected. I was the same myself, guys, when I was your age – letting down the tyres of my Geography teacher's car, for example. He wasn't happy, I can tell you. Especially when he lost his licence for two years.'

Dwayne snorted up his sleeve.

'But the thing is, guys, Mrs Tubbins is upset, so we'd appreciate it if we could tidy this place up. Can you do that, guys?'

They started to half-heartedly clear things away and Davidde went back to his book. Lyndon noticed this.

'Sir? Sir?'

The Head took no notice of Lyndon.

'Sir? Mostyn?'

Still no reply.

He tried again. 'Evsie?'

'Yes, what is it, young Lyndon?'

'Why isn't Davidde helping, Sir? He started it. He chucked books at us when we came in. I don't see why we got to tidy up all this mess when it's all his fault and he's just sitting there reading. Like a girl.'

The Head walked over to Davidde.

'OK, son, muck in, then. Lend a hand, is it?'

Davidde felt his face going red.

'But I didn't do anything.'

'Come on, son, many hands make light work.'

As the Head spoke to Davidde, the gang left their tidying and sidled up to him.

'Come on, Dai, you done it as well,' said Dwayne.

'Ay, don't be sly, mun,' grumbled a few other voices.

'They're right, Dave, don't be sly. The more of us

there are helping out, the quicker we can all get on and forget all about this. Or do I need to speak to you in my office?'

Davidde was in new territory now, because he had never been remotely in trouble in his life. It wasn't that he was a goody-two-shoes, he just hated conflict and hated the idea of letting anyone down, especially the people in charge of him. Being in trouble just didn't come naturally to him.

'Do I, son? Need to speak to you?'

Davidde was aware of Lyndon Lyons' gang smirking as he felt his face burn with shame and indignation.

'The boys here have been dull, but at least they've been honest. Are you going to be honest, or are you going to be sly? Because I won't tolerate that, not in my school.'

Davidde got up and started to put books away angrily, keeping his eyes down as he felt them becoming watery. The last thing he needed was for that lot to think he was crying. He needn't have worried, because as he put the books back the rest of them slunk out of the library and up the field for a cheeky fag before the bell went for afternoon lessons.

When he finished he was surprised to find that the Head was still there.

'What's your name, boy?'

'Nippers. Davidde Nippers.' It was the first time he'd ever spoken to a teacher without using Sir or Miss to finish his sentence.

'Well, listen to me, Nippers my boy, I'm watching you. I'm going to be watching you very closely.'

And with that, he left.

There was no sign of his father when he got home from school, so Davidde did his homework and went next door to see Mr Leighton. Mr Leighton had spent three hours that afternoon polishing his pristine silver Volvo, but now he was stood at the window of his living room with his binoculars to his eyes, furious. There was always something in his life that could make him furious. His current source of anger was the group of boys riding scramblers on the waste ground at the foot of the mountain, known locally as the Rec. It wasn't clear whether it was the noise he objected to, the fact that they were churning up the ground and making it unsafe for walkers, or that they might hurt themselves. Nobody knew. All Mrs Leighton and Davidde did know was that he was furious.

'Look! Look! They're at it again! No tax or insurance, I bet. They should be doing their homework. Why aren't they doing their homework, Davidde?'

'Maybe they finished it.'

'Finished it! Finished it! They've been out there for hours! Finished it! I phoned the police at four o' clock and there's been no sign of them.'

When he wasn't beside himself with anger, Mr Leighton had quite a placid nature. He didn't really say much, but when he did, it often had very little connection with the current topic of conversation. Once, Davidde and Mrs Leighton had been talking about dogs, and Mr Leighton sat up and said, 'China's got to change.' Another time, Davidde had been a bit sad and Mrs Leighton was doing a great job of raising his spirits. From out of nowhere, Mr Leighton looked into the distance and shouted, 'Don't play the banjo, play the violin!' and left the room. It made going next door interesting at least.

When Davidde got back to the house his father was back from work. He was at the kitchen table reading the paper, smoking and drinking cider. He didn't look up as Davidde came in.

'Where you been? Next door with Miseryguts, is it?'

'Aye.'

'What was he moaning about today then?'

'The boys on scramblers down the Rec. He says they're a nuisance.'

His dad shook his head.

'He's moaning cos there's boys on scramblers. What does he expect? Next thing he'll be moaning that water is wet, or that wood burns. Boys and bikes go together like fish and chips. When I was your age…'

Davidde had heard this before. When Ralph Nippers had been Davidde's age, he'd been the best scrambler in the valley. He'd take on all-comers, and he wouldn't just beat people, he would send them for fags. (Davidde never really understood what sending people for fags actually meant, but the way his father said it, it sounded quite impressive.)

Davidde was also aware that he was a bit of a disappointment to his father. He'd never taken up scrambling or sport the way his father had, and this meant that they didn't have much to talk about. This hadn't been a problem when Mam was alive, because she wanted him to do well at school, but then she got cancer and died, and Davidde and his father had to get by on their own. Most of the time things were fine, but occasionally Davidde felt he should get in trouble at school just to keep his father happy. His father was famous in the area for being expelled from school on his last day because he used a water pistol to squirt pee over the headmaster. The thing was, Davidde didn't like getting into trouble and he liked doing the work. It was something his father could never get his head around. He considered telling his dad about the new headmaster and how he'd spoken to Davidde earlier that day, but even thinking about it made his cheeks feel hot and his eyes watery. He'd just leave it. Anyway, the last thing he wanted was to give his father a chance to go down to the school and start ranting and raving. That would be awful.

The rest of the evening passed quietly. They had egg and chips for tea and then his father went out to the Club. This left Davidde alone. When it went dark he set up his binoculars to look at the stars. He had a tripod and had managed to fix his binoculars onto it to give himself a steadier view. He had saved up for a proper telescope and Mr Leighton was helping him choose one. Mr Leighton was an expert when it came to surveillance.

Davidde focused on the Andromeda Galaxy. It was incredible to him to be able to see something that wasn't just outside the Solar System, but was outside the galaxy. Now this was the sort of thing that sent his head for fags.

He was asleep before his dad got back. He dreamed he was down the Rec, watching Lyndon and Dwayne and the boys messing around on their bikes. They were doing wheelies and their own special scrambler jousting, where they would race at each other and try to spit on the rider racing towards them. They were having a whale of a time, and they didn't notice Davidde gazing down on them. It was then he saw the Black Rider for the first time.

Riding a gleaming silver scrambler with the shiniest chrome exhaust ever, dressed head to toe in the blackest leather, the Black Rider ascended the crag overlooking the Rec, and then stopped at the very top. Lyndon and the boys, even Dwayne, stopped riding and spitting for a moment to admire the powerful faceless figure above them. The helmet was black, the visor revealed nothing. The Rider slowly raised a gloved hand and pointed.

At Davidde.

Then the figure beckoned him over. Davidde couldn't believe he'd been picked out over the other boys. He was uncertain, and a bit scared, but he obeyed anyway. He made his way over, through Lyndon's gang, who looked on in awe. The rider was utterly still, looking down like a statue carved from granite.

Davidde climbed up the crag, and faced the rider. When he was level, the rider put their hands to the sides of the helmet and slowly started to raise the visor. Inside seemed to be a perfect blackness. The Rider, head bowed now as if in prayer, had the visor completely open. The helmet was raised and Davidde was able to see that instead of eyes the rider had a pair of…

'Prawn balls, Dai? I got some Chinese for us, butt.'

His father was back, and was sitting on Davidde's bed, sharing a takeaway with him. He seemed a bit happier, as he often did when he came back from the pub.

'Bit early to be kipping, isn't it?'

'Tired, Dad.'

Davidde tried to eat a prawn ball, but it was making him feel ill, as if he was eating an eye. But whose eye? And what message did they have for him?

His dad left him to get some rest, but Davidde found it difficult to relax, and had a fitful night's sleep, although he didn't dream of the Black Rider again.

At least not that night.

3

It was Art again. Dwayne Tight had got hold of a knife and was hacking lumps out of the table. When he had a row, he tried hacking lumps out of Ceri Fuss. When he had a row for that, he started hacking lumps out of himself.

Miss Pughes-Pervis had explained the two-year course to the class and had started them off on their first project, which involved the class drawing a still life of a flattened hedgehog. Then she took Kaitlinn and Davidde to one side to talk them through the first part of their course.

She opened up a booklet with the list of projects in it.

'Obviously you need to keep all your planning sheets and preparatory work and put it together with your final piece to make it a proper job. Now then, here we go – choose one from the following list of five!'

She clapped her hands together with excitement.

'One: Phlegm through the Ages. Hmm – interesting – suggests sculpture to me. Two: Horsepower – that could be one for you, Kaitlinn!'

Kaitlinn loved horses, and with her longish face and sizeable nose, Davidde sometimes thought she'd started to look like one. Miss Pughes-Pervis, though, didn't suggest Kaitlinn try a self-portrait.

'Three: The Joy of Wrecks. Sounds like landscape to me. We could organise a trip to the seaside or something. Four: The Sky at Night. That could be one for you, Davidde – you like stars and planets and Astrology and all that.'

'Astronomy, Miss.'

'Whatever. Five: Pterodactyl Soup. That sounds a bit weird to me – and I'm an Art teacher!'

She turned to her A-grade students and asked them what they thought.

'Horses,' said Kaitlinn, thinking that she could use her own horse, Alfie, in some way.

'The Sky at Night,' said Davidde. He was going to buy the telescope this week. Mr Leighton had been helping him choose one online, and they'd almost come to the end of the decision-making process.

'That's great. Well, you can start on a few planning sheets, and it would be lovely if you could come back to me a week today with something to show me, and with some idea of what your final piece is going to be.'

They went to different tables to start gathering a few ideas. Kaitlinn worked with her back turned to Davidde.

'I'm drawing Alfie,' she said.

'I'm sketching Uranus,' said Davidde.

Kaitlinn rolled her eyes.

'That's exactly what I mean by pressure. Every day. Every stinking day.'

Davidde didn't have a clue what she was on about.

'What you drawing, butt?'

It was Dwayne. Miss Pughes-Pervis had had to separate him and Ceri because he was trying to bite her. He was only joking, he said. But Miss thought it was safer if they sat apart. Davidde was concerned about having Dwayne sat next to him, but he tried not to show it. The only times

Dwayne had spoken to him before were to call him a tool or a spanner when Davidde dropped a pass in rugby.

Davidde showed him his planet.

'That's good that is, butt.'

Davidde asked Dwayne what he was drawing.

'An SMX-600, butt. My dad's getting me one this weekend.'

Davidde looked at it and tried to work out what an SMX-600 was. It looked like it had been drawn by a hyperactive chimpanzee, high on cheap squash.

'Can you help me with the front wheel, butt? And the 'elmet.'

From Dwayne's questions, Davidde was able to make out what the drawing was meant to be. It was a scrambler with the rider leaning back, doing a wheelie.

'Nought to sixty in five seconds, thirty brake horsepower, top speed sixty-eight miles per hour! Motocross, boy, racing on dirt-bikes!'

He leaned back on his stool as if he was riding it, his hands on the handlebars, his right hand revving the throttle.

'Mwaaaaaah! Mwaaaaaaaaaaaaah!' he shouted at

the top of his voice, imitating the sound of the engine, changing pitch as he changed gear.

Davidde tried helping out with the front wheel and helmet.

'Thanks, butt, that's tidy, that is.'

He paused, then shouted, 'Miss, Miss, look what I done!'

The lesson passed, and Davidde was surprised to enjoy sitting next to someone for the rest of the lesson, even if it was Dwayne, who never called him a tool or a spanner once.

Back at the house after school, Davidde was in his bedroom counting up his money. With his last pocket money from his dad, he had just enough to buy the telescope and tripod Mr Leighton had helped him choose. He'd been keeping all his birthday and Christmas money for the last couple of years, and now he was ready. He counted it one last time to make sure he was right, and then went round and knocked on the door. Davidde was going to give Mr Leighton the cash so he could order with his card. There was no answer. Davidde tried again. This was very strange – Mr Leighton was always at home in the afternoons.

Mr Leighton was at home, but he was in his greenhouse tending to his tomatoes. He loved it in there. He couldn't hear boys on their dirt bikes, he wasn't getting annoyed by his computer playing up, it was just him and his tomatoes. It was his favourite place, the only place where he found inner calm. He didn't know what he'd do without it.

Mr Leighton was getting a little older and deafer and Mrs Leighton was out getting a few things for the house, so she wasn't there to let Davidde in. Davidde wondered what to do.

As he did so, he saw something that, before today's Art lesson would have been a worrying sight.

It was Dwayne Tight, pushing a scrambler up the street. Normally Davidde would have avoided eye contact with him, but now he felt confident enough to talk to him. Dwayne pushed the bike past him.

'Alright, Dwayne?'

'Alright, butt?'

'Where you going?'

'I'm selling my bike like, got a new one coming this weekend. I'm taking it down Phil's to see how much he'll give me for it.'

Phil's was where Davidde's father worked. Davidde thought for a few seconds. A strange idea started forming in his mind. Davidde walked after Dwayne.

'How much do you expect to get for it?'

'I'll take anything round an 'undred.'

Davidde felt the money in his pocket. It was madness. What would he do with Dwayne's old scrambler? But then again, who was the Black Rider? Maybe it was a sign.

'I'll give you a hundred for it.'

'Who? You?'

'Aye. Me.'

'Where you going to get that money from?'

To Dwayne's amazement, Davidde produced it from his pocket and counted it for him.

'You sure about this, butt?'

'Never been surer.'

Davidde looked at the bike and scratched his head.

'I've never done this before – I'll need a few lessons.'

'I can help you, butt, no problem.'

Dwayne turned the bike around so they could go back down the Rec.

'How do I start it?'

'Stick this on your bonce for a start.'

Dwayne gave Davidde a helmet. He put it on and pulled down the visor. He started to feel different.

'I'll throw in a penknife as well – you never know when it'll come in handy,' Dwayne said. He got Davidde to sit on the bike.

'You're not really meant to do this on the pavement but it's OK because there's no one around. Just be careful. It's in neutral – start her up.'

Davidde didn't know what to do.

'Kick starter – right foot, mun.'

The engine was running.

'Now rev the engine – right hand, butt.'

The scrambler roared. Telescopes weren't this exciting.

'Pull in the clutch – left hand. Right, put it in gear – use your foot!'

Davidde put it in gear, but he wasn't prepared for the raw power of Dwayne's bike. The back wheel spun, and because Davidde was leaning back the front wheel reared up and he fell off. The bike powered on down the pavement by itself.

Dwayne was laughing hysterically when a figure came out of one of the houses, with the bike going straight for him.

It was Mr Leighton!

He saw the bike just in time and threw himself into the nearest garden. He was in a rose bush shouting 'HOOLIGANS!' at the top of his voice. Dwayne was chasing after the bike, which had fallen on its side. His face was red with laughing, tears streaming down his face. Davidde got up and ran after him, hoping Mr Leighton wouldn't recognise him with the helmet on. He ran after the bike and Dwayne, and felt an elation he'd never felt before. Dwayne was already on the bike and got Davidde to jump on the back. They rode away down to the Rec so Dwayne could start Davidde's education properly.

Davidde spent the next couple of hours with Dwayne. It turned out that Dwayne was a good teacher. By the end of the session Davidde was able to balance and ride quickly without falling off, and was doing a decent wheelie. He put the bike in the garage that backed on to the alley behind his house. He walked into the kitchen to find his father smoking and drinking cider again.

'Where've you been?'

'Down the Rec. On my scrambler.'

His father stopped mid-drag.

'You what?'

'I've been down the Rec on my scrambler.'

'Shut up, mun.'

'I have – it's out the garage – come and see.'

His father followed him; he was staggered to see the scrambler. Davidde wasn't sure, but thought he saw his dad's eyes go slightly glassy.

'Dai, Dai, I never knew. I ... I ... would have bought you one years ago. But you were always doing daft things like – well – reading books, and doing homework. What sort of a father am I?'

'It's alright, Dad.'

Ralph looked at the scrambler, and thought back to when he was Davidde's age, racing and getting into scrapes with his bike. It was great. Davidde *could* be a chip off the old block after all.

'Let's go back inside. You can have a glass of cider with your old man.'

Ralph put his arm round his boy's shoulder and led him proudly back to the house.

His father told him stories he'd heard many times, but it didn't matter. It was great to see his father so happy, and to be happy with him. It didn't take long before Ralph said that it was a shame his mother wasn't here to see him. At this point Davidde was concerned things were going to get a bit sad – he couldn't cope when his father drank too much and started crying, so he made his excuses and took himself off to bed.

'Thing is, butt, I loves her.'

Davidde found this hard to understand. Dwayne was sitting next to Davidde again in Art, because he'd tried sitting next to Ceri Fuss but got moved because he'd poked her in the eye.

'I want to say something nice, or do something tidy, and I go to do it but then I pull her hair or I bite her. I can't explain… You won't tell the boys, will you?'

'Why don't you want them to know?'

'They'll make fun. They can be hellish nasty.'

Davidde knew how hellish nasty they could be. But he was surprised that they'd be nasty to one of their own. They seemed thick as thieves most of the time.

'That's why I picked Art. I can't stand drawing, but none of the others took it so it means I can have a break from the boys making fun of each other's family. I remember once Muppet asked Froggy if his gran would give him piano lessons, and he knows she ain't got no arms!'

'Don't worry, I'm not got going to say anything, Dwayne.'

'Thanks, butt.'

Normally after getting home from school Davidde would have done his homework, but that night he'd arranged to meet Dwayne down the Rec to get a few more lessons. The other boys in Lyndon's gang would be in football training, but Dwayne preferred messing around with bikes. Davidde was improving rapidly, and Dwayne enjoyed helping someone develop an interest in something he loved.

An hour later, Davidde noticed Lyndon's gang in the distance. This made him feel uncomfortable, and he noticed it made Dwayne uncomfortable as well. Davidde thought the best thing to do would be to go home. He had work to do by the next day anyway.

'Who was that on your bike, Tighty?' asked Froggy.

'That was that Davidde Nippers kid, wasn't it?' said Muppet.

'Nuh.'

'Yeah, it was…'

'You fancy him!'

'I don't!'

'Yes you do, look at him blushing!'

'I'll tell you who's gay, Froggy.'

'Who is, then? Tell me.'

Dwayne had to think for a minute.

'Er … your pants! No, your mother's pants – your mother's knickers. No, your mother's sweaty fat knickers!'

The boys groaned at Dwayne's efforts. Dwayne didn't find making original insults very easy.

Davidde sat at his desk to do his RE homework. He resented having homework for a subject that he hadn't chosen, and he'd also given up believing in any sort of god after his mother died. However, he sat down to do it because he liked the teacher, Mr Muffin, and doing homework was something that he did. He'd never think about not doing it.

But as he sat there, toying with his penknife, trying to follow a dreary worksheet about Saint Denzil (the patron saint of tarpaulin) he drifted off to sleep at his desk, and he was back down the Rec. Lyndon Lyons was there, taunting Davidde, saying he rode like a girl. Davidde challenged him to a race, and Lyons asked him how far. Davidde looked up, and in the distance could make out the Black Rider, motionless on the crag.

'As far as that,' he said, pointing at the crag.

Froggy started them off, but Lyndon cheated anyway. After a bit he got cocky, and turned round, flicking the wide Vs at Davidde. He hit a pothole and veered across Davidde's path. Davidde expertly avoided him and took advantage, reaching the Black Rider two lengths ahead of Lyndon. Lyndon took it very badly.

The Black Rider beckoned Davidde over. Davidde rode over and stopped.

The Black Rider slowly raised the visor.

All was dark.

As it opened, Davidde could see that amazingly, instead of two eyes there were two...

'Scotch eggs! Dai, I got us some scotch eggs. For a change, like.'

It was his father back with some tea.

4

It was Assembly. The head was on stage before anyone arrived. He stood behind the lectern as the hall filled and as everyone sang the hymn.

'Thank you, Mr Mantovani, for that lovely rendition of 'All Things Bright and Beautiful', and thank you, Year 10, for that memorable dubstep breakdown halfway through. We shan't forget that in a hurry.'

He leaned over with his elbows on the lectern and his right hand on his chin while Year 10 unplugged the drum machine and put down their recorders.

'They tried their best. And that reminds me a bit of Wilfred Sprocket. He was a hell of a boy was Wilf, up to allsorts. And he had a gift. Like Year 10 by there. Except he wasn't a musician, he was a dancer. To be exact, he was a tap dancer. Now I know what you're thinking – how on earth do you dance on a tap?!'

Nobody was thinking that, especially the staff, who rolled their eyes as one.

'Well, I'll tell you. Tap dancing is a special kind of dancing where you have a metal piece on your shoe, and it makes a sound like this.'

He moved from behind the lectern and flicked his right foot. It made a clop sound on the stage. Then he flicked his left foot, and that also made a clop sound.

'Watch this now,' he said.

He started by slowly clip-clopping around the stage, flicking his feet and waving his arms energetically. Then he got faster and Miss Jones and Mr Graves, the Games teachers, exchanged glances, shaking their heads slowly with their mouths wide open in horror. Their mouths gaped even more as the Head approached the lectern and pulled out a cane which he held over his head, and then tapped on the stage as a part of the performance. After two minutes of energetic hardcore tap, the Head clapped his hands and stopped with his arms spread, breathing heavily through his sweaty face, eyeballing his audience, waiting for the applause.

When there was none, he put down his cane, wiped his face with his hanky and took his place back behind the lectern.

'Tough gig,' he mumbled, and went back to his notes.

'Now, even though Wilf had a gift, he didn't have it easy. In school all the boys who liked football and rugby used to make fun of Wilf, especially as he had sold his togs so he could buy tap shoes, and he had to wear these in Games lessons. Well, you can imagine, can't you...'

The Head mimed Wilf acrobatically slipping over in the mud.

'It was like Bambi On Ice. And as if it wasn't bad enough being picked on by the other boys, he was picked on by the staff as well. Teachers then weren't as nice as they are now. They didn't know what to do with a boy that wouldn't stop tap dancing.

'Anyway Wilf left school and joined a local dance troupe, then he got noticed and taken to Cardiff. He danced all over Wales, and then started dancing in London. He was the talk of the town – no one danced like our Wilf!

'Now, I know what you're thinking – where could he go from there? What happened to Wilf?

'Wilf got invited to dance in New York, in Harlem, the capital of tap. He would sail over in a cruise liner and amaze everyone with his remarkable butt-leg coordination. What could possibly go wrong? What indeed?

'I'll tell you what. The cruiser he was travelling on was the Titanic and he drowned. He did manage to get into one of the lifeboats, but nerves got the better of him and he started tap dancing in fright and went through the floor – it was only made of balsa wood. Nobody ever saw him again, but his memory lives on, and I think he can be an example to us all – not in the way he effectively killed himself and everybody else on the lifeboat – but in how we should all use our gifts to achieve our potential. Which brings me to this young man here...'

The Head pointed at a stranger no one had noticed before. He was standing at the side of the hall where the staff watched over their form groups.

'I'd like to ask him to the stage, because he has an announcement that could help some of you achieve your potential, like Wilf. Hopefully without drowning…'

The man made his way to the front.

He didn't just walk, he swaggered, rolling his shoulders and pouting his lips. He had a pork-pie hat on and shades, even though it was belting down with rain outside. He was wearing the skinniest possible jeans, so tight that he clearly found it hard to bend his legs. With his massive trainers, it looked like he was walking on two mutant golf clubs. He was carrying an expensive smart phone which he tapped as he walked. He carried on tapping on the stage while everyone waited for him. He finished, looked at the phone, laughed at what he had written then put it in his pocket. He wore a crumpled suede jacket, and a shirt under it that was open just above the belly button. He didn't look like he was from the area.

'Hi. I'm Nathaniel Grimes, yeah?'

He didn't sound like he was from the area either. Almost everything he said was a question.

'You all like television, yeah? The telly, the TV, the goggle-box, whatever you call it in this hole, yeah?'

Some nodded.

'Well, I'm from TV, yeah, and I'm gonna put one of you on it.'

He took off his shades and started chewing one of the arms.

'Who wants to be on telly, yeah?'

Many hands went up.

'But not just anyone. Who likes singing?'

Loads of hands went up, including Eira Scoggins, her eyes wide with excitement. She'd auditioned for a TV talent show before. She was convinced that the only reason she didn't get selected was that she'd bitten one of the other contestants for looking at her funny.

'That's great. But I'm not looking for singers.'

Eira Scoggins pulled back her lips and bared her wonky teeth at Grimes. He put his shades back on.

'Who likes dancing, yeah?'

A few hands went up uncertainly.

'Yeah? Well, that's so last year I can't believe you'd admit to it. Sad.'

He took his shades off again, now that Eira had put her teeth away.

'Now, I know there's something you guys like, something real, something now. Who likes bikes?'

Hands went up again.

'I'm not talking about sissy pushbikes here. Anyone can ride one of them. I'm talking about off-road, I'm talking about scramblers, I'm talking dirt-bikes, I'm talking Motocross!'

Lyndon and the boys looked at each other. Slowly Lyndon raised his arm, and as he did so the rest of his boys did the same.

'That's it, yeah, the real men!'

Davidde felt that he shouldn't really put his hand up. He'd only had his bike a little while, and wasn't really used to riding it. He worried what the teachers would think now that he had a bike, and he worried that others would think he was trying to fit in.

But then he thought again. He'd bought the bike, it was his, he rode it, so he was into scrambling. Everyone had to start somewhere. He was fed up of worrying what everyone else thought. He was going to put up his hand.

So he did.

Straight away he was aware of Lyndon looking over and saying, 'Look at Dai', and sniggering, but Davidde didn't care. He was committed.

'That's great, lads, yeah? Now, I can't say too much about it at present, but next week we're having a race, and whoever wins is going to take part in the show. Come and see me after assembly, yeah, and I'll give you the details, yeah? Yeah.'

The Head walked on and said, 'Thank you very much Mr Grimes, yeah?'

He was very impressionable.

After assembly Lyndon and his boys crowded around Grimes and bombarded him with questions. They were normally so quick to make fun of people who volunteered to do things for school that not many people volunteered to do anything at all. Davidde thought about how they were usually so keen to look cool, and yet here they were acting like five year olds. Davidde would have been warmed by the spectacle if he hadn't been afraid they were going to turn around and beat him up.

'Guys, guys, yeah, like I said I can't say too much about it. Just read the flyer, yeah, and I'll see you next week, yeah? Yeah.'

He handed out glossy postcard-sized flyers to all of Lyndon's gang, and to others standing around, and as he made his way to the yard he put one in Davidde's hand.

Davidde read the flyer.

**ARE YOU TOO COOL
FOR SCHOOL, YEAH?**

AND SINGING AND DANCING IS FOR GIRLS, YEAH?

DO YOU LIKE BIKES, YEAH?

(AND THAT'S REAL NOISY ONES,
NOT SISSY ONES WITH PEDALS, YEAH?)

**BRING YOUR BIKE TO
THE REC NEXT FRIDAY 7PM**

The flyer was snatched out of his hand. It was Lyndon.

'He's gorra scrambler and now he thinks he's hard, boys.'

They all laughed. They'd stopped being five year olds and started being a danger again.

'I might have a go next Friday, why not?'

'I might have a go next Friday,' mimicked Lyndon, using a girl's voice. 'Tell you what, Dai, I'll give you a race tonight, boy, see if you're up to it. After school, down the Rec.'

Davidde felt himself blushing, but he had to meet the challenge.

'OK, why not?'

Lyndon moved closer to him, raised his hand and tapped Davidde's face three times, then held his cheek between his thumb and finger.

'I've heard your old man was a bit good in his time.'

Davidde looked down at the floor, nodding, feeling his eyes stinging.

Lyndon moved in even closer so he only had to whisper.

'But you don't ride like him. Do you know who you ride like, butt?'

Davidde shook his head.

Lyndon got so close Davidde could smell his faggy breath.

'Your mother. Your dead mam.'

Their eyes met, then Lyndon pushed Davidde's face away and laughed as it bounced off a double-glazed window. The others looked at Davidde with disdain as they all dispersed and went to first lesson.

Davidde went to English with Mr Rastud. When he saw Kaitlinn flouncing up to the teacher with two sides of perfect handwriting he realised he hadn't done his homework. This was a new sensation for Davidde and he feared the worst.

Mr Rastud had set the work at the end of the last lesson. It had been a disjointed lesson that had started on poetry, then went into a twenty-five minute rant about the misuse of the word 'decimate'. He used pictures of stickmen on the board and covered the front row in spit as he went red with furious anger. He clenched his fist and grimaced as he slammed the board. He would have continued, but caught sight of his watch. He fell back into his chair and put his head in his hands.

'Do me a story. Eight hundred to a thousand words. By Thursday.'

'What about, Sir?' someone asked.

Mr Rastud looked out of the window for a long time.

'How can I tell you what your story's about? It's your story.'

'I'm rubbish at stories, Sir.' It was little Matthew Pie. 'Can you give me a title or topic or something?'

'Ducks.'

'Ducks?'

Matthew's face crinkled with confusion.

'What kind of ducks?'

'Hopeless ducks. They've forgotten how to swim and fly. They are rubbish.'

'Why have they forgotten?'

'They're always drunk.'

'Why are they drunk?'

'Look, I could tell you, but I'd have to decimate you after. Work it out for yourself.'

Next lesson Matthew seemed to have worked it out quite well. Mr Rastud asked him to read out his story. It turned out that the ducks lived near a brewery and it was leaking beer. Because of their erratic behaviour they became celebrities in the town, and then got taken on a tour. But because they were away from the factory they weren't drunk anymore, so people got bored with them. The evil man who'd taken them on tour decided that he could get his money back by selling them to be eaten, but they escaped in the nick of time and flew into duck rehab. The story was called Cold Turkey for the Ducks.

Davidde and the class had been lulled by Matthew's story and it got a well-deserved round of applause. Mr Rastud went round a few more people, listening to opening paragraphs, or in some cases the whole story. Davidde tried to make himself as insignificant as possible. He thought that if Mr Rastud didn't call his name out, he could slip away at the end of the lesson and say he forgot to hand it in. He was scared Mr Rastud would find out he hadn't done his story, and he'd have a row, and get detention, and have a letter home (not that his father would be that bothered, it was just the shame of it). There would be countless awful things if Mr Rastud found out that he hadn't done his homework.

Then the unthinkable happened.

'OK, Davidde, let's have yours.'

Davidde didn't know what to say. Should he start with an excuse, or should he maybe pretend to have some sort of fit to distract attention? He felt his cheeks go hot and looked down at the floor. He decided he might as well be honest.

'I forgot,' he mumbled, and he fully expected Mr Rastud to go into one of his mighty rages. He expected to be picked up and thrown across the class, to be humiliated and to be made an example of in front of his peers. He expected to be moved into one of the less able sets.

'No problem. Bring it in when it's finished. Right, who's next? Janet Parpins – let's have it.'

'My story is a true story. It's called The Most Scared I Ever Been.'

'Please carry on, Janet.'

'The Most Scared I Ever Been. The most scared I ever been was when me and my family was on a nudist beach and a wasp flew straight up my…'

'Stop!' shouted Mr Rastud.

'…nose.'

'That's alright. Carry on.'

Davidde couldn't believe it. He'd worked himself up so much, but there was nothing to worry about. He started to understand how people got to ride bikes and do things outside school that annoyed Mr Leighton so much. They never did their homework! It was so obvious. He decided that he could devote more time to being good on the bike by spending less time on his homework. He wasn't going to stop doing it altogether; he'd just be a bit more selective about it. He pulled himself together and enjoyed the rest of the lesson.

Last lesson was Art. Davidde was surprised and a bit annoyed when Dwayne came to stand by him as they queued up outside the door. Davidde couldn't say for sure that Dwayne had been laughing when Lyndon was picking on Davidde, but it wasn't as if he'd tried to stop it either.

'Ow, butt. You really racing Lyndon tonight then?' he asked.

'Yeah. Why?'

'The thing is, Lyndon isn't very good. If you listen to him, he's the best in the world. But he doesn't like anyone passing him on the inside. He panics and lets you through – I've never understood why. And you can do it on your bike as well – it's powerful enough.'

Miss appeared at the door.

'I've got something a bit different for you today. I've prepared something for you, something to make you think about things. It's what we call an installation. Art doesn't just have to be pictures, it can be something you can move around and look at from different angles. I call this Exploding Rabbit Hutch.'

And that was exactly what it was. Miss had blown up a hutch, and somehow found all the bits and put them back together. Except that it wasn't the hutch as it was before it was blown up, but the hutch as it was exactly half a second after the explosion. It was at head height with pieces suspended on strings from the ceiling so that they moved slightly, and light refracted through the spaces between the pieces of wood and chicken wire. Even though the hutch hung silently, there was a real sense of violence and movement.

Ceri Fuss looked worried.

'Don't worry, Ceri,' said Miss. 'I know what you're thinking, and no, there wasn't a rabbit inside it when I blew it up.'

Davidde wasn't really into three-dimensional art, but even he had to admit that this was impressive, though he didn't see himself doing something similar.

'Why not, Davidde?' asked Miss.

'I think I feel safer on paper, that's all.'

Kaitlinn really liked it, and she returned to her sketches enthused. Davidde spent the lesson hiding from Miss because he didn't have anything new to show her.

Davidde found that he was nervous on his way back from school, but not unbearably so. Who was Lyndon to speak to him like that? Davidde would show him.

His dad was still at work so he went next door to see Mr Leighton. Mrs Leighton let him in and gave him a glass of squash. Mr Leighton was at the window with his binoculars, his forehead corrugated with anger.

'Look! They're at it again! On their bikes! Riding them!'

'Let's have a look, Mr Leighton,' said Davidde, and Mr Leighton handed the binoculars over. Davidde looked over to the Rec. He saw Lyndon and the boys, riding, larking around. He shivered. He wasn't in their league. But he had to go through with it. And what if Mr Leighton recognised him? He was difficult to live next door to as it was, but if he knew Davidde was over there he'd have the police up all the time. Davidde would just have to keep his helmet on.

He gave the binoculars back to Mr Leighton.

'I've got to go. I'll call in tomorrow,' he said as he made his way to prepare for the battle.

When Davidde got to the Rec, Lyndon was astride his bike, eating a bag of crisps and a bar of chocolate at the same time, while smoking heavily and drinking from a can of pop.

'Look who it is, boys.' Lyndon pointed at Davidde's black shiny helmet that was too big for his head. 'It's Darth Vader.'

As he spoke the mixture of crisps and pop and chocolate splattered from his mouth. The others laughed and pointed too.

'I'm going to rub your helmet into the dirt,' he said as he crushed his can and dropped all his wrappers on the ground. Davidde approached.

'Ready, butt?' asked Lyndon.

'Aye,' said Davidde. 'What's the course?'

'Down to the burned-out car. The one that used to be red. Then go over to the burned-out car that used to be black. Then go round the burned-out car over by there.'

'What colour did that used to be?'

'Nobody knows. It's always been there.'

Davidde wanted to tell Lyndon how daft that sounded, but he didn't dare.

'You goes round that car and you comes back by here. Three times. Ready?'

'Yes.'

'Start us off then, Craig.'

Craig started to say, 'On your marks, set, go,' but Lyndon had already left by the time he opened his mouth. Davidde got into gear and went after him.

The first lap he was just trying to keep up. At one point Lyndon was riding standing up on the seat, showing off to the boys. Davidde managed to catch up then, so Lyndon sat back down and raced properly. Davidde just managed to avoid a deep pothole in the middle of the track towards the end of the first circuit and he thought he was holding his own. By the time they'd done one lap, Davidde was aware that he had much more power and speed on the straights, so he decided to wait to take Lyndon on the third lap. He kept Lyndon in his sights and chipped away at his lead.

He was just behind at the start of the third lap. He got down to the car that used to be black and then pulled out to pass Lyndon on the long straight up to the car that used to be red. He found he couldn't make it, but then he remembered what Dwayne had said – he doesn't like anyone passing him on the inside, he just panics and lets them through. As the corner hurtled its way towards them, Davidde braked and then got himself between Lyndon and the turn.

And it worked! Lyndon did panic and Davidde nipped in before him. He increased his lead on the straight, and as he eased away he couldn't help looking back and seeing the snarl on Lyndon's angry face – he looked so unhappy!

But in looking back, Davidde failed to spot the huge pothole he'd avoided earlier. The front tyre went straight down it and there was nothing Davidde could do as he went flying over his handlebars, flipped in the air and landed on his back looking up at the sky.

Lyndon raced past him gloating loudly and went on to finish the course to cheers from his gang. He rode back over to Davidde.

'Unlucky, Darth, butt. Like I said, you race like your mam.' He rode back to his gang, who wanted to celebrate by setting fire to something. Davidde thought he'd better disappear fast, before they decided to set fire to him.

Davidde cursed himself for looking back at Lyndon during the race – if he hadn't turned around he would have won! But he was also happy that he'd been able to compete, and he was pleased he'd given Lyndon a scare. Maybe with a bit more practice he could beat him next time, and he vowed that he would put the hours in. He would look for books and magazines that could help him get better. He could speak to his father. He'd been pretty decent in his time, even Lyndon knew that.

Davidde made his way home, and furtively put the bike in the garage behind the house, making sure Mr Leighton wasn't lurking around any corners. He let himself into the house. His back was hurting from where he'd landed so he reckoned he'd run a bath. There were no lights on but there was a note on the kitchen table.

'Davidde – late back tonigth – pasties in frij – herd you was racing – how did you do? Dad'

Davidde was puzzled, and not by his father's scattergun approach to spelling – that was something he was more than used to. His dad never stayed out, especially mid-week, or if he did, he didn't plan it. It just happened. And how did he know about the race? Davidde hadn't said anything. It was all very mysterious.

Davidde had his pasties as he ran the bath. The hot water hurt the grazes on his back, but in a way they felt like war wounds and he felt he had earned them. After he had dried himself he was too tired to do his French homework – that could wait. He tried reading an astronomy book in bed as a way of researching ideas for his art project, but found it boring and fell asleep. He was losing interest in stars and planets.

He dreamed of the Black Rider again.

5

The dream didn't come right away because Davidde fell into a long, deep sleep. He'd been very tired. But towards morning he dreamed about his race with Lyndon. It was happening in slow motion. Lyndon was standing up on the seat of his bike, but everything was going too slow and Davidde couldn't catch up. Then Lyndon was doing a headstand, and Davidde still couldn't catch up. Then Lyndon was riding the bike with his head on the seat and opening and closing his legs, showing off to his friends and winding up Davidde. Then he was eating a bar of chocolate, drinking a can of pop and lighting up and smoking two cigarettes. Even Davidde had to admit that was impressive.

The Black Rider was there, arms folded.

Davidde tried as hard as he could, and found himself drawing level with Lyndon. Again he tried pushing past using the bike's power, and again he failed. Then he remembered Dwayne's advice, and went for the inside. Lyndon (who had by now abandoned his selection of snacks and fags, and had re-assumed a more orthodox riding stance) looked on in horror as Davidde passed him again.

Davidde was filled with elation, and he was doomed to make the same mistake again!

As he rode on, he couldn't help but turn around and catch Lyndon's displeasure. He'd never felt anything like it – the feeling of being ahead, the smell of the petrol, the sensation of speed, it was fantastic! It felt even better this time!

When he looked back in front of him, he was heading straight for the pothole, but this time the Black Rider was stood in it, wagging a gloved index finger at Davidde. He tried again to avoid the inevitable, but it was impossible. Davidde slammed into the Black Rider and the pothole and again he went flying.

When he came round he was looking up at the sky. He was waiting for Lyndon to come over and tell Davidde he rode like his mam. But the Rider was there, looking down at him. Lyndon was riding over from the finishing line, ready to gloat. The Black Rider got up and stood between Lyndon and Davidde. Lyndon stopped and looked at the Rider, then at Davidde, and then back at the Rider, and this time he thought better of gloating. He rode off.

The Rider came back and knelt by Davidde. The visor lifted.

Davidde couldn't see the face, but where there should have been two eyes, Davidde could see two...

'Cadbury's Creme Eggs! Dai, I got us some Cadbury's Creme Eggs for breakfast – for a change, like. I called in the shop on the way home.'

His dad was sitting on his bed. He'd brought some mugs of tea up as well. He seemed happy.

'Where've you been?' asked Davidde.

'Out.'

Ralph cleared his throat and shifted on the bed. Normally Davidde wouldn't ask any questions if he saw his dad was uncomfortable, for fear he would get angry. This morning though Davidde thought he'd find out.

'Where though?'

Ralph cleared his throat and then looked hard into his mug.

'Boys. Cards.' He coughed. 'Drinking. Tired. Sleeping.'

He bit the top off his chocolate egg and chewed like a maniac, then smiled, then remembered where he was.

'Anyway butt, what about the race last night?'

'How did you know about it?'

'Saw Lyndon's old man in work yesterday. I told him you'd kick his boy's arse. How did you get off?'

'Lost.'

'Shame that. I can't stand Lyndon's father.'

'I can't stand his son.'

'What happened?'

Davidde went into detail about the race. His dad stopped munching and looked down, apparently deep in thought. Then he started talking with an eloquence that surprised his son. Ralph's stumbling grunt was replaced with a quiet, low-pitched, thoughtful way of speaking that Davidde found hypnotic. He asked questions that made him rethink the events of the race, especially stuff that had happened in a split second. Ralph reflected on his son's answers and made suggestions about what to try next time.

The tea was cold when they finished.

'I'll come and watch you next time, Dai. I should have been there last night.'

'It's alright, Dad. I'm glad you didn't see me come off.'

'Everyone does, son – it's part of the process. If you've never fallen off a bike you've never been on one properly. That's what your gran used to say to me whenever she had to take me to casualty, and she was right.'

They got ready for work and for school and left, feeling closer than ever.

As Davidde got to the school gates he was lucky not to be knocked over. He was thinking about the race and hadn't been looking where he was going, and the next thing he heard was the sound of a car's horn. He jumped out of the way and Miss Pughes-Pervis flashed past him in her big black car. In the passenger seat was Mr Rastud, white-faced and staring straight ahead of him with a look of terror. You could tell that he'd seen some terrible things sharing a lift with Miss, but that morning he seemed more frightened than usual.

Art was first and it was lively. Dwayne had some surprising news for Davidde.

'Lyndon wants a rematch, butt. Tomorrow down the Rec. What'll I tell him?'

'Tell him aye.'

'Good. I'll tell him. I hope you smash him.'

'Why?'

'Last night he started acting like a chicken and he knows that I'm scared of birds.'

Davidde didn't know what to say and went back to his drawing.

Dwayne found it hard to concentrate. He was too busy looking at Ceri Fuss. She was sat next to Kaitlinn sharpening her pencils and lining them up so they were exactly parallel to the edge of the desk. Davidde could hear Kaitlinn telling Ceri about the Suffragettes. He didn't know much about them, but he wasn't that interested in any bands from the sixties.

'I loves her,' said Dwayne.

'Why don't you give her something?'

'Like what?'

'I don't know. Something in a box. Girls like that sort of thing, I think.'

Davidde looked over at Ceri to see what sort of thing she'd like to get in a box. He couldn't tell, but what he could tell was that Kaitlinn was looking at him. And she didn't like what she saw. She was cutting up some bright red paper with a pair of shiny scissors, her face a tight scowl. Davidde tried to move so that Dwayne was between him and her. He tried adding to his stars and planets project, but it just wasn't working. He'd started avoiding Miss so that she wouldn't see how badly he was doing. She'd never had to speak to him before about not doing his work, so it was easy for Davidde to hide. Whenever she'd start coming around the room towards him he'd feign an interest in something on the wall, or in one of the Art books on the shelves, and he would say he was doing 'research'.

She was coming round now. Davidde nipped off to look at some of the work on the wall. There was a new piece up. It was called 'Homage to Salvador Dali'. It featured a pair of scissors sticking out of a horse's eyeball.

It was by Kaitlinn.

Miss had made it round to Dwayne and was asking him how things were going.

'Look, Miss, this is rubbish, this is.'

Dwayne showed her, and even he knew that she wanted to agree. Dwayne was probably one of the worst drawers ever to put pencil to paper. Every line he made was a disaster. When he drew an eye, you could tell he'd tried drawing something round, but that was all. It could have been a tin; it could have been a sombrero. When he tried to draw a nose, it could have been a boomerang or a coathanger. Everything was wrong, and then when they all went on the page they never fitted together. The relationships were truly comical, so that people would laugh out loud at his work, thinking it was some marvellous joke. But it wasn't. It was just Dwayne's artistic ability.

'It's a positive start, Dwayne.'

'Admit it, Miss, it's rubbish, innit?'

'No, Dwayne, you're trying really hard.'

'You don't have to lie, Miss, I can take it. It's rubbish, innit?'

Miss Pughes-Pervis surveyed Dwayne's picture. She sighed. 'Yes, Dwayne. It's pathetic, frankly. I'm not going to tell you any more lies; you're hopeless at Art. I've seen slugs with more aesthetic ability than you.'

'Thanks, Miss.'

Miss sat where Davidde had been sitting. To make herself feel better she started look through Davidde's work. But apart from a few early sketches, there didn't seem to be anything there. She called him over and asked him where the rest of his work was.

'In the house. I'll bring it in next lesson.'

'The thing is, I'm depending on you and Kaitlinn not to let me down. Kaitlinn's got some really good things done already, but I haven't seen anything from you. I think you're the only people I've taught anything at all to in this year.'

Davidde felt bad for lying.

'Next lesson, Miss.'

The rematch with Lyndon came around soon enough. Davidde was surprised to find that even though he felt nervous, he really wanted to race Lyndon again. He felt that it was his duty, not just for himself, but for his father. Ralph, when he was about, would ask Davidde what he would do in different situations, and Davidde found it helped him visualise events in the race. He'd gone round the course so many times in his head he felt he could do it with his eyes shut.

He spent less time in the library as well, less time waiting for the night to come. The night had been when he had felt safer, in his house looking at the stars, or next door with Mr and Mrs Leighton. But now he spent more time wandering the school in the daytime, and found he had more people to say hello to. He took more notice of faces and less of the floor. As he walked up the narrow stairway by the canteen, with two of Betty's legendary rock-hard baps in his hands, he felt pretty pleased with himself. That's when he felt the wetness on the top of his head, and when he heard the mocking laughter.

He saw six or seven faces peering over at him from the floor above, where Lyndon and the boys used to hang around. Davidde had forgotten the risk involved in climbing these stairs at the wrong time. The wrong time was now, when they were holding one of their spitting competitions. It was said that Pickle could lower eight inches of phlegm from his mouth, pick up a fifty pence piece with it and suck it back up to his mouth without using his hands. One of the faces was Pickle's. Davidde put his hand to his head, it did feel quite sticky.

'Terrible rain we're having, boys,' said Lyndon, and they laughed again. Davidde saw Dwayne laughing along with them.

'You coming down the Rec tonight then?' asked Lyndon.

'Yeah. You scared I'm going to beat you?'

'Just thought you might be washing your hair, that's all. See you later, loser.'

Lyndon and the boys ambled away, but Dwayne was at the back of the pack, though he couldn't bring himself to look back at Davidde. Davidde waited for them to go, then went to the toilets to wipe off whatever was on his head.

He wanted to drive his bike over Lyndon's face and leave permanent tyre marks on it; the sort of thing he'd seen in cartoons, only this time for real.

He would get his revenge, he thought, bent double with his head under the drier. Oh yes, he would get his revenge.

Davidde was a little late getting to registration and the rest of the class had left. He apologised to Mr Lunt. Mr Lunt did a double take and pointed at Davidde's head.

'Nice hair, butt. That's proper trendy, that is!'

Davidde left without saying anything more. He hated it when teachers were sarcastic.

'There's nice your hair is, love.'

Even Mrs Leighton was being sarcastic now!

'It's proper trendy. I never thought you were trendy, I thought you were a geek. Tell him his hair's looking nice, Charles.'

Mr Leighton had his binoculars trained on the Rec. He didn't look up.

'Aye, it looks antique.'

'I said I thought he was a geek, not he looked antique. I think it's very nice, Davidde.'

Davidde had been aware that people had been looking at his head all afternoon. It unsettled him, but not enough to put him off the race. He was understanding what people meant by getting focused. He was running different scenarios around in his head, and he was applying solutions to potential problems that could crop up later. He was also thinking about Dwayne walking away with the rest of Lyndon's gang. Why didn't he say anything? Why didn't he act like a friend? He'd helped Davidde so much recently, and Davidde liked to think he'd given in return.

'I've called the police. We won't be seeing any old scramblers tonight, I'm sure,' said Mr Leighton triumphantly.

We'll see about that, thought Davidde, as he made his excuses, and went next door to get ready for the big race.

Davidde made sure not to turn up too early. When he got there, Lyndon's crew were gathered around him. Craig was relaxing him by rubbing his shoulders, and Pickle was entertaining him by doing tricks with phlegm. They were a very confident group, except for Dwayne, who was skulking about on his hands and knees, doing some last-minute work on Lyndon's bike.

'Here he is, boys, Darth Vader.' They all laughed.

'Alright, butt,' said Davidde, 'so I got a black helmet that's too big for me. It wasn't funny first time.'

'Oooh, listen to her, boys.'

Davidde found himself not being scared of Lyndon any more, but actually being fed up with him. He thought about how Dwayne had said he was annoyed with Lyndon too.

'Shall we get this done then?'

'After you. Ladies first.'

Davidde led the way to the starting line. He looked at Lyndon. Lyndon drew level with his visor up.

'Gonna ride like your mam again?'

Davidde thought he should say something cool. It was well known that Lyndon's mother wasn't too sharp. He thought about taking advantage of this by saying something like, 'At least my mother never gave me Ralgex sandwiches on a school trip.' (Lyndon's mother had actually once mistaken an open pot of muscle rub for lemon curd before a school trip to London, and Lyndon spent most of the day in Hammersmith Accident and Emergency having his scalded tongue seen to.) Davidde put his hand to his chin to help him think, but as he did, the race started and Lyndon was off to a flier. Davidde quickly engaged the clutch but he was already miles behind. He cursed his stupidity.

Lyndon had a huge lead. Davidde gained on him slowly, but at the end of the first lap Lyndon still had the edge. He wasn't showing off this time, so Davidde found it hard to catch up, but at least he felt he'd earned a little bit of respect. On the second lap Davidde's power started to count and he was right behind Lyndon. He followed in his slipstream and waited for the third lap to make his move. He was enjoying himelf again. He could tell Lyndon didn't like having him right behind. His frontrunner's movements were jerky and showed signs of panic. It was just a matter of time – take him on the inside, like Dwayne said.

But as they started on the third lap, Davidde lost a little bit of concentration. He became aware that his father was stood on one tip, looking down on him, clapping and shouting encouragement. On another, Davvide thought he could see the Black Rider, motionless on the big black bike. He felt under pressure to perform. He blinked hard, shook his head and decided to make his move. He made ground and got within passing distance and went for the inside, but Lyndon blocked him off!

Davidde lost quite a bit of speed, he wasn't expecting Lyndon to do that – he didn't last time. He waited till the next corner, but Lyndon blocked him again. They were on the final straight – Davidde had to use his power now, that's all he had left.

He told himself not to look round if he pulled ahead – that's how he lost last time!

He opened up the throttle and his bike took off. He pulled level with Lyndon. He was tempted to turn sideways and look Lyndon in the face as he pulled clear, but he fought the feeling and concentrated on what was in front of him. No potholes, no danger. He spotted Lyndon's bike through the corner of his eye as he pulled clear, till he was only aware of the Lyndon's front wheel. He was ahead, but he couldn't shake the front wheel, it was still there!

He was dying to look but he couldn't.

The wheel was still there!

The line was approaching – he had to look!

He could only take a quick look.

He looked. He couldn't believe what he saw.

He had to look again!

The front wheel was there, but that's all there was. Lyndon and the rest of the bike were nowhere to be seen.

Davidde looked to the front to check for holes and slowed down as he approached the finishing line. He allowed himself to look behind him. He could see Lyndon's bike on its side, the front twisted and bent. Lyndon himself had flown over the front of the bike, his head landing in a pothole, his body sticking up straight out of it, his legs waving in the air. Davidde laughed and pulled a wheelie as he crossed the line.

Winning felt fantastic!

His father ran to him and there were tears in his eyes!

'Dai, Dai! I don't know what to say – I just feel so – proud!'

Davidde didn't know what to say either. This was the first time his father had felt proud of him. For all the work he did in school, he realised that his father just didn't get it. This sort of thing he understood.

'I mean, you would have beaten him anyway, but when he went over his handlebars, well ... I know it's bad, but it was, like, the funniest thing I ever seen in all my life.'

'I'd better see how he is, Dad.'

'Aye, you do that.'

Davidde rode over. Lyndon was out of the hole now. He was sat on the floor, winded.

'You better not be coming here to gloat.'

'No – I've come to see you're OK. You OK?'

'Aye, butt. I would have beaten you then. I'll

beat you in the proper race, you remember that. You had a lucky break this time.'

Lyndon was OK. Nothing was his fault, as usual. Davidde thought that if Lyndon had checked his bike properly he wouldn't have had a problem. He had enough experts to help him after all.

Dwayne walked over to Davidde with his hand out. He looked sheepish.

'Well done, butt.'

Davidde couldn't really understand why Dwayne was congratulating him. It was hardly like Lyndon's boys to be magnanimous in their leader's defeat. Davidde shook hands with Dwayne. He found it weird.

'Well done, butt, you did real well.' As they shook hands Dwayne tried to signal something at Davidde with his eyes. 'Real good like.'

'Did you see anyone looking at the race?'

'Only your father.'

'Did you see anyone on a black bike. Black leathers?

'Can't say I saw anything like. Anyway, you done well.'

Davidde could feel something in Dwayne's hand.

'Real tidy. Time for you to go though now, innit.'

'Thanks Dwayne. That means a lot, butt.'

Dwayne went back to the group. Davidde looked down at his palm. Dwayne had left a wingnut in it.

The wingnut that held the front wheel on a scrambler.

Ralph was pushing Davidde's bike up the crooked alley behind their house, on the way to put it in the garage. When Mr Leighton's kitchen window came into view, Davidde stopped his father.

'What you doing?' asked Ralph.

'I don't want Mr Leighton to see me.'

'Why not?'

'He'll go nuts. He was helping me look for a telescope, but I spent all my money on my bike. And he spends most of his time phoning the police complaining about the kids down the Rec on bikes.'

'And he doesn't know that you're one of them?'

'Correct.'

'That's hilarious, that is.' Ralph took a moment. He looked into Davidde's eyes. 'He needs to learn that sometimes things change. Sometimes we change. Sometimes some things can change us, deep inside.'

'Are you feeling alright?'

'Er, yeah, I'm fine. Look – I might not be around much this weekend. Will you be OK?'

'What's happening?'

'Nothing, I'm just not going to be around much, OK?'

'OK, I've got plenty to be getting on with.'

'Tidy.'

6

The week passed quickly and the proper race came around soon enough. Davidde had decided to use gel in his hair, after he realised that he was getting genuinely positive messages about how Pickle's mucus made it stand up on its own. It wasn't sarcasm at all. He didn't get much further with his Art project, though he had managed to avoid Miss for another week. Dwayne had said nothing about his sabotage of Lyndon's bike either – it was something to be left completely unacknowledged. Dwayne had been friendly in Art lessons, but Kaitlinn was going the other way completely. Davidde stayed out of her way. He also seemed to be seeing less of his dad – he was hardly in at nights at all. Davidde wondered how much poker one man could play?

Lyndon had also kept a low profile. Whether it was the ignominy of losing, or just of flying over his handlebars and landing head-first in a hole, it was hard to tell. Either way, Davidde didn't see much of him until the posters went up.

They appeared one day, plastered all over the school.

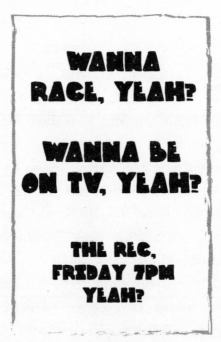

WANNA RACE, YEAH?

WANNA BE ON TV, YEAH?

THE REC, FRIDAY 7PM YEAH?

There was great excitement. On the Tuesday before the race, Ceri Fuss walked over to Davidde in the yard at breaktime.

'Oh, my gawd, like I've heard you are wicked on the bike like.'

Davidde didn't know what to say.

'I'm alright like,' he said.

But he was chuffed. This sort of thing didn't usually happen to him. And Ceri Fuss wasn't the only one. Younger boys in Year 7 looked at him in awe. Davidde felt great.

On Wednesday, he was teasing his gelled-up hair in front of the mirror in the toilet before Art. Pickle came in by himself and did a double take when he saw Davidde. Pickle went straight for Davidde's throat. He grabbed him and held him against the cold, wet wall.

'Listen, Dai, I'm only going to say this once, pal, so listen carefully.'

Davidde knew there was nothing he could do. Over the years he'd learned to keep his head down and not to be in the toilets at the wrong time. This had kept him safe. Now he realised he'd been taking a few too many risks. This was the price of arrogance.

'Listen, Dai.' There was something heartfelt and pleading in Pickle's pained blue eyes.

Davidde braced himself for the punch to the stomach and the application of mega-hold phlegm to his hair. Pickle was going to pay him back for giving him the idea for wearing gel.

'I like your hair.'

'Thanks. It's gel this time, not your mucus.'

'You've got to beat him on Friday. I know you think I like him, but I don't. I only do tricks to stop him making fun of my boy-boobs.'

He paused.

'I can't help it if I've got a fuller figure. That's what my mam says.'

Then Pickle left, slamming the door behind him.

Five seconds later he came back in.

'I came in to have a slash,' he said.

Art was looking to be another long game of cat and mouse for Davidde, except that Dwayne had handed him a lucky break. Again, Davidde didn't have anything to show Miss Pughes-Pervis, and he wanted to make sure he had clear escape routes to his left and to his right so Miss couldn't trap him into having a conversation about his lack of coursework. It wasn't long till half-term, and there were only a few weeks to get everything done before the moderator came in.

Dwayne sat down by Davidde.

'I took your advice.'

Davidde couldn't remember giving any advice.

'You know, about giving her something special. In a box, like.'

Dwayne went under the table and produced a bag. This was surprising, as he never brought a bag to school. He rummaged around inside it, and brought out a metal tin that had once held shortbread. Davidde asked him what was in it.

'Watch this now,' he said, before finding a thick permanent marker and scrawling 'sori i carn wait till valentines' on the tin. He crept his way across the room to where Ceri Fuss had been sitting. She was looking for ideas on Miss's bookshelf, so Dwayne left the tin in her workspace on the table. Then he crept his way back.

'What's in it, Dwayne?'

'Can't tell you.'

'Well, it seems very thoughtful. I never took you for the romantic type.'

Dwayne got agitated as Ceri wandered back to her desk, with a heavy book on Salvador Dali in her hands. His face was screwed up and he was breathing heavily. His hands were balled into fists that he rubbed against his trousers.

Ceri sat down and inspected the box. She read the message on it and looked around. Dwayne kept his head down and tried to look like he was working. Ceri shook the box and listened. She put the box back down and tried prizing open the lid. It was hard for her to open. She tried again; the lid flew across the table and the quiet of the art room was shattered by the lid crashing on a desk, and then Ceri's piercing scream.

Ceri was on her feet – there was something green on her shoulder. She waved her arms and then it was on her head! She was screaming and shaking her head to get it off. Arming herself with the Salvador Dali book she started hammering at the table.

'What was in there, Dwayne?"asked Davidde. Dwayne held his sides as he laughed and he tried to say, 'Frog!'

Ceri was a well-known animal lover, but in her shock she had flattened the frog. It was running down the book cover and spine like the melting clocks on the cover of the book. This irony was lost on Miss, Dwayne and most of all Ceri, who had to be taken to the sick bay for the rest of the day to recover. Dwayne spent the day in the

Deputy Head's office, writing but he thought it had been worth it. Davidde was delighted that the fuss Dwayne had created had taken most of the lesson to sort out, and he didn't have to worry about his artwork for another week.

Davidde didn't feel like it, but he called in with Mr Leighton on the way home. He'd been avoiding him because he felt uncomfortable with his double life, humouring Mr Leighton and his irrational hatred of scrambling and scramblers, and then being one the scramblers his neighbour so detested. Mrs Leighton let him in, but he didn't get the usual welcome. He followed her into the kitchen. For a change Mr Leighton wasn't at the window, but was sat down at the kitchen table fuming about something in the paper instead.

'Mad, it's gone, the world. The world's gone mad,' he said.

'Have a biscuit,' said Mrs Leighton.

'I can't, I'm too annoyed about those Mongolian bats.'

'I wasn't talking to you, I was talking to Davidde. Have one when you've calmed down a bit.'

'My tea will be cold. And everyone knows there's no point having a biscuit with cold tea.'

'Well ... well ... stick it up your backside then,' said Mrs Leighton and she ran upstairs crying, after she'd thrown a biscuit at Mr Leighton's head.

Davidde had never seen them like this before. They'd bickered plenty of times, but he'd never heard Mrs Leighton upstairs sobbing before and he found it a bit awkward. Mr Leighton carried on reading the paper, mumbling. Davidde followed Mrs Leighton upstairs.

'Sorry, Davidde, love. How are you? How's school going? We don't see you as much as we used to.'

Davidde thought about school. It had been great, mostly, but not in the way she was thinking. He hadn't kept up with any of his work, work he would have done if he'd called in on them more often. He thought he'd better not mention that and make things worse.

'Everything's fine, Mrs Leighton.'

'How's your father? Haven't seen him in a while either.'

'I haven't seen much of him myself to be honest, Mrs Leighton.'

She sniffled.

'Sorry, Davidde,' she said, 'but sometimes I can't cope with him. He can be such a ... pig.'

'He has been quite grumpy lately.'

'I mean, most of the time he's fine, and I realise that I'm lucky. It's hard for your father, and for you, losing your mother like that.'

Davidde thought about Mr Leighton downstairs, not apologising, just muttering to himself. And then Davidde realised something. For a long time he'd felt guilty about how Mr and Mrs Leighton had been so good to him over the years, especially since his mother had died. The times they'd cooked for him and helped with the homework his father couldn't help him with, the times they'd made him cups of tea, the times he'd looked at stars with Mr Leighton. He realised, though, that they'd got something out of this as well – they enjoyed the company, and he didn't have to feel guilty about it. He'd felt guilty about so many things – like being a burden on his father, about being bullied in school, about not having things to say to people.

He realised that he didn't have to feel guilty about every single thing.

'OK, Mrs Leighton, I'll try and talk to him,' said Davidde. As he walked back down the stairs he realised he didn't have a clue how to do this, but he would give it a go.

Mr Leighton was at the window with his binoculars, fuming. His face was red and he was shaking.

'Miscreants! Blaggards!'

'Hiya, Mr Leighton. What's happening?'

'Oh, the usual, you know. The world going mad, idiots on the Rec and the police not taking a blind bit of notice.'

'Mrs Leighton doesn't seem very happy.'

'Don't worry about her, she's never happy.'

Davidde thought that he wouldn't be very happy if he was Mrs Leighton either, but he didn't say it.

Mr Leighton put down the binoculars. He stared hard at Davidde.

'And how's school going?'

Davidde felt very uncomfortable. It was as if Mr Leighton knew the truth. He went to scratch his head. He felt the gel in his hair.

'Well...' said Davidde. Right on cue there was a tap at the window. It was his dad.

'Come back to the house, mun, I got us an Indian. Hiya, Charlie, how's things?'

Mr Leighton went to the door with Davidde to let him out.

'I was saying to young Davidde now,' said Mr Leighton, 'we haven't seen much of him lately.'

'I'm not surprised, Charlie,' said his dad. 'He's been too busy practising.'

'Practising?'

'Yeah, practising.'

'Practising? For what?'

'For the big race this Friday.'

'What big race this Friday?'

'Down the Rec. On his bike.'

Davidde heard Mr Leighton's binoculars smash on the wooden floor.

'You'll get a good view from here.'

Not with smashed binoculars he wouldn't.

He pointed at Davidde.

'You ... how ... since when ... why?' spluttered Mr Leighton.

'Come on, Charlie,' said Ralph. 'He's young, he's got a bike and he's having fun. He's not hurting anyone...'

'BUT IT'S AGAINST THE LAW! HE'S TOO YOUNG! HE'S NOT STUPID LIKE THE REST OF THEM! HE'S NOT STUPID LIKE...'

He stopped.

Ralph was much closer to Mr Leighton now. Davidde saw him draw up close to Mr Leighton's face, looking angry and talking quietly.

'No, go on. What were you saying?'

Mr Leighton looked away. Davidde was worried his father was going to hit Mr Leighton.

'Not stupid like I was, is it? Was that what you were going to say?'

Mr Leighton squirmed where he stood, but didn't back down completely. 'Having fun is he? Having fun. Like Stuart Davies was having fun.'

Ralph drew back as if he been punched. He seemed to lose a foot in height.

'Stuart Davies ... Stuart Dav ... now he was stupid ... he was stupid...'

Ralph backed away from Mr Leighton's door, pointing at Mr Leighton as if he was threatening him, but visibly upset as he moved backwards towards his own house.

'He was stupid. He was definitely stupid. But he was definitely having fun.'

Obviously, Davidde had to know who Stuart Davies was. Ralph was only a few steps ahead of his son, but when Davidde got into the kitchen he had a can of cider in front of him and he was sucking furiously on a cigarette.

'Let me tell you about Stuart Davies,' said Ralph

quietly, looking into the distance through the kitchen window. 'Stuart Davies was mad. I know people say that about people who are a bit funny, or people who act a bit dull to get attention, or people with red hair (and he did have red hair, by the way), but Stuart was seriously mad. We were in the same year in school, and I used to sit by him. Well, I did while he was still cleaning his teeth.'

'Why did he stop washing his teeth, Dad?'

'We had a race down the Rec one day, and it was on a day when he'd forgotten to clean his teeth. We'd been making fun of him all day, then we had a race and he won. I beat him the next night, and he'd remembered to clean them that day. The next time he had a race, he didn't clean his teeth, and guess what happened?'

'He won?'

'Correct, son. He became convinced that cleaning his teeth took away his scrambling skills. He was like that Samsung from the bible, only with furry orange teeth instead of hair. That's when I had to stop sitting by him. I was starting to feel sick all the time in lessons.'

'So were you best friends?'

'Oh aye, we did everything together. Riding bikes, seeing girls, fighting with boys from up the Park. Everything, mun. But he was a little bit older, a littler bit bigger and usually a little bit quicker to do things than me.'

'So what happened to him?'

'The more he won, the more sure he was that he couldn't lose. He began to think that he was invincible. He started doing dull things, stupid things...'

'Like what, Dad?'

'Stunts, long jumps, stuff like that. We'd get all these younger boys to lie in a line and he'd set up a ramp and fly over them.' His voice became hoarse. 'It was obvious someone was going to get hurt...'

'Go on, Dad...'

'We were going for a new record, but we couldn't find enough boys. I mean, we had seven volunteers but we needed ten. We found another three but they didn't want to do it and they were crying and weeing themselves and running off, so we had to try something else. One of the boys suggested that we light a fire and Stu could leap over that. Even Stu thought that sounded a bit too dangerous. Then somebody found some plastic guttering, and we decided to fashion it into an archway. We set it at the top of the ramp so Stu could come through it. Then someone found some blue plastic sheeting. We could stretch it over the arch and Stu could come flying through it, like someone off TV. It was going to be perfect.

'It was then I think I heard the sirens.'

He had a drink and thought for a moment.

'Stu didn't want to get stopped, so he went back and revved the bike. The sirens were getting louder, and there was someone running down the hill shouting at the top of his voice. Stu revved and revved, and then he was off. He was going really fast with his head down, to make himself as aerodynamic as possible. Then, I don't know why, he sat back and made himself as tall as he could. He was showing off most probably. Anyway, he totally misjudged where the guttering was.'

He looked Davidde in the eyes.

'I know plastic guttering doesn't seem very solid, but when you drive into it at sixty miles an hour without your helmet on, I can assure you it is sturdy enough. It caught him right under the nose. His head stayed still for a second while his teeth flew on ahead of him, like brown wonky marbles. It was a terrible thing.

'He was on his back, there were sirens and there was shouting. I didn't know what to do. Everyone else pegged it, and I wanted to as well, but I also wanted to see if Stu was OK. I feel ashamed to this day about it, but I rode off as well, and left Stu there.

'When I was safe, I looked back, and I saw an amazing thing. Remember I told you about Stuart and his oral hygiene problems? Well, imagine that with blood and loose teeth and cut lips. And remember I told you about the angry shouting man? About how annoyed he was at us? Well, the old man gave Stu the kiss of life. It's the most selfless thing I've ever seen. Definitely the most courageous.'

'Who was the shouting man, Dad?'

'Have a guess?'

Davidde thought for a moment, while Ralph flicked his eyes towards next door.

'Mr Leighton?'

'Explains a lot, don't it?'

And then it was Friday.

The school was abuzz. There were a few youngsters who were going to take part, but everybody knew that really it was going to be Lyndon versus Davidde. Dwayne wasn't in school that day, but Davidde was used to not seeing him on the day of a race. Dwayne was undercover with Lyndon's gang, and hopefully he'd get to sort Lyndon's bike like he did last time. Davidde had confidence in how Dwayne was operating, though it did make him feel uneasy. After all, technically, it was cheating.

The day passed quickly enough, and Davidde actually got some decent work done in Art while Dwayne wasn't there to distract him. Miss was still concerned about Davidde, but he did enough to keep her at bay. Kaitlinn was experimenting with clay and her work was showing a lot of promise.

Back in the house, his father was back before him.

'Davidde, I got something for you, for tonight.'

This was unusual. His father wasn't usually one for giving presents outside birthdays and Christmas, and he wasn't very keen on it then.

'I been up the attic. They're my old boots and gloves. I would have got you my helmet but there was a pigeon nesting in it. Made a hell of a mess, he did.'

They were black and scuffed and undeniably cool.

Davidde thanked his father and put them on. He looked at himself in the mirror and seemed to grow two inches. He felt bullet proof.

'Get out there and show that Lyndon what you can do. You show him. And his father. Especially his father. He's the best mechanic I know, but my God, just try spending five minutes with him. He makes you evil, mun.'

At the Rec there seemed to be thousands of people. There was a desk to sign up at. Nathaniel Grimes, the strange man from Assembly, was there.

'Here for the race, yeah?'

'Aye,' said Davidde.

'Sign this, yeah?'

'What is it?'

'Health and safety, yeah? It just means if you get hurt or killed I don't have to do anything, yeah? Or failing that, not much, yeah? You gotta fill in a form for everything nowadays, yeah?'

'Yeah?'

'Yeah. See you on the start line in ten minutes, yeah?'

'Yeah.'

Davidde found it hard speaking to someone who asked him a question even when they were telling him something. He tried to focus before the big race. He looked to see if Dwayne was working on Lyndon's bike. He'd been so crafty the last time. Davidde felt bad thinking Dwayne was a bit too dull for that kind of behaviour, but he'd done well. Hopefully he would have worked out a similar scam for tonight, Davidde thought. He was surprised at how calm he felt, too. He made his way to the line, and surveyed the course with his visor open.

He was confident, but not over confident; he was controlled, but not too controlled; he was cool, but not too cool.

It was then he tasted the mud and felt earth stinging his eyes. Lyndon had thrown a clod of turf in his face.

'Get used to it, butt, you'll be tasting a load more of that when you come off!'

As he cleared the muck from his face, Davidde tried desperately to think of something he could say to Lyndon to get back at him, but nothing would come. He decided it would be better to embarrass Lyndon by beating him in the race, rather than bragging now and looking stupid later if he didn't win. He would do his talking with his bike (and with whatever Dwayne had done to Lyndon's bike).

There was a two-minute warning. The bikers gathered on the line, the spectators gathered around the course. Everyone knew that, till very recently, this would have been a walk in the park for Lyndon. He had bossed the course for years, but now there was a new kid on the block, a new kid with a funny name who people weren't scared of. Almost everyone was willing him on. They munched on their cheap burgers and hot dogs from the vans that had arrived in force, taking advantage of the hundreds who had come to spectate.

Davidde felt part of something big. Almost nothing happened in the village on a Friday night, at least not when it was light and most people were sober. Davidde thought about how far he'd come – not long ago he'd have been in the house on a night like this, reading books about stars, or even doing homework! What had he been thinking? This was great, but he didn't want to stop here. He had to beat Lyndon, and he had to get into the competition. He just had to.

He saw his father in the crowd, and he saw the Black Rider looking down from a knoll above the crowds.

This was it. Engines running.

The Big Race.

'You all ready, yeah?'

Grimes was speaking through a megaphone, standing in front of the starting line with a chequered flag in his left hand.

'I know you're all ready to go, but there's a few things we need to go over, yeah?' He pointed at one of the riders. 'You, son, you're not in Ben Hur, you're not allowed to have spikes coming out of the sides of your bike – hop it, yeah?'

'Boring,' grumbled the anonymous rider.

'No bumping, no tickling, no gouging, no fish-hooking, no biting, no petting, yeah? Apart from that you're fine, yeah?'

The nine riders left nodded in agreement.

'On your marks, get set, go, yeah?'

Nobody moved. They weren't sure whether he'd started the race or not.

'Like now, yeah?'

And they were off.

Davidde wasn't used to riding in such a pack, so he thought it best to stay out of trouble for the first bend. He was right, the first three to the corner all went for the tightest racing line and took each other out. Then there were only six left in the race, and he was aware that two of those left were clearly overawed and were driving like old men on a Sunday afternoon. He could keep in sight of Lyndon and take him on the last lap, when whatever Dwayne had done to Lyndon's bike would start to take effect.

On lap two he decided to get closer to Lyndon, who was in the lead. He opened up the throttle to take the rider in second place. But whenever Davidde tried to pass him, he'd pull aggressively in front of him, causing him to brake and lose ground on Lyndon. It didn't make any sense – why would someone try harder to stop Davidde than to win the race themselves, when the only prize was for the winner?

The rider turned his head round momentarily. Davidde glimpsed the smirking face of Craig Jib. Now it made sense! Craig was there to stop Davidde from beating Lyndon, and it was working – it was almost the end of the second lap!

Craig mouthed, 'Like your mam!' at Davidde and blew him a kiss.

If Craig Jib had concentrated on racing rather than gloating, maybe Davidde would never have got past him. But he couldn't help it – that was the type of person he was. Davidde seized his chance and eased himself through the chink of light Craig had left clear by taking his eye off the road in front.

Now all that needed to happen was for Lyndon's bike to start failing. Davidde wondered about what Dwayne had done. Would Lyndon go flying over the handlebars again? Would the handlebars come off in his hand? While he thought about this, he realised that he wasn't gaining on Lyndon at all. He thought he should try and pass Lyndon rather than just wait for something to happen.

He was just behind him, but Lyndon hugged the inside line, and Davidde didn't seem to have the power to go the long way round. There were now only three corners to go and Davidde was still in second. When would Lyndon's bike break down?

At the corner, Davidde thought he saw some room, but Lyndon closed the space down and Davidde was shut out again. Two corners to go!

On the straight he was exactly level with Lyndon. Davidde tried not to get distracted, but he couldn't help turning to look at Lyndon just for a moment. It was a good job he did, because Lyndon was reaching out for Davidde's handlebars. He got hold of them and started wobbling, trying to throw Davidde from his bike.

They went round the penultimate corner like that, with Lyndon shaking Davidde's handlebars, and Davidde trying to keep himself steady and get Lyndon's hand off his bike. Lyndon's bike seemed to be losing power and Davidde realised that because Lyndon had grabbed hold of his bike, Davidde had the inside line for the final corner – all he had to do was stay on his bike and he would win!

But Lyndon still had hold of his bike. On the final straight, Davidde tried to pull clear, but he was still tussling with Lyndon. The pair veered off towards the few trees on the course and Davidde ducked as he saw a low-hanging branch. Lyndon didn't see it as he grappled with Davidde's handlebars, but he felt it as he got it full in the helmet. His bike shot off without his weight and finished the race before Davidde, but it didn't matter because Lyndon was lying under the trees, pounding the ground with his fists as Davidde finished the race and went on to do a lap of honour.

Davidde felt like a hero for the first time in his life. There was clapping and cheering, and he was presented with fizzy pop on a white podium. The man from TV said he'd be in touch and his father was sobbing with joy.

The Black Rider wheelied off up the mountain. It was all a bit of a blur.

Davidde thought he'd better get his father home before he embarrassed himself any further.

1

It was Monday morning assembly. The Head was on stage. The curtains were drawn behind him. There was a sense of anticipation in the audience.

'Now then, boys and girls, we've got a very special assembly this morning. I know what you're thinking. You're thinking, how will he humiliate himself this time? After all the upsetting stories and after the tap dancing, how's he going to embarrass himself now? Well, I'll tell you. I'm not. I'm not because for once this assembly isn't about me. It's about a very special young man who is amongst us now. And I think you know who I'm talking about.

'But let's go back a few steps. Let's go back to the beginning. The beginning, when I started here as headmaster. Now I know how you feel when you look up at me, you look up at me and you wonder how I got to be such a figure of authority and yet such a "cool guy", as you young people say. Well, it's not easy, I can tell you that for nothing, but as I said, this isn't about me so I'll save that for a different assembly.

'When I started here, I needed to get a feel for the place, so I spoke to people, and I watched, and on the whole I really liked what I saw. I saw vitality, I saw energy, I saw a lust for life – with most of you.

'But there was one young man, and he was so different. Dull, lifeless eyes, walking round looking at the floor, not talking to anyone. I'm sure most of you felt the same as me when you saw him walking towards you on the corridor. You'd think, "Here he comes, Boring Nippers, I hope he doesn't start banging on about stars again" or "Hell's bells, it's Boring Nippers, why doesn't he just throw himself off a cliff or something?"

'Now don't get me wrong – I agree that all work and no play makes Jack a dull boy, but I also believe that all play and no work makes him a complete liability. It's all about finding a balance. It was great that Davidde was doing all his homework, but he needed something else.

'Luckily for us all, he's changed. He's still doing

his homework – in fact, he's doing so well in Art that he's doing his GCSE a year early. Think about that, boys and girls!'

Some pupils clapped, and Davidde could feel Miss Pughes-Pervis' eyes boring into his skull. He looked up at the ceiling to avoid her gaze.

'Now, apart from his academic ability, he's developed another string to his bow – dirt bike racing. On Friday he won a competition, and now he will represent us on Valley TV's *Search for a Scramble Star*. Three big races over the next three Thursday nights that will give Davidde the chance to win this…'

The headmaster raised his arm and looked behind him as the curtains opened to reveal a brand new motocross bike, a shiny Pegasus DC-5000 L. It glistened under the lights, and there was even some dry ice rolling across the stage. Davidde knew this was the prize but he wasn't expecting to see it this morning, and both Dwayne's and Davidde's eyes widened in astonishment.

Davidde had to have it.

After assembly, the man from the TV explained to Davidde how the competition worked. His company was launching a hyper-local channel for the area, and one of the first shows would be with a dirt-bike knockout challenge. There would be three races – one in Abercwmffrwmpan, one in Glynwinci and the final in Maesunig. They were also borrowing an idea from wrestling, where the contestants would have characteristics and personalities, so that people who didn't care that much about scrambling could get some sense of drama from the show.

'You won't be using your usual name, yeah, we'll give you a new name,' said the man from the TV.

'What will my name be based on?' asked Davidde.

'My media team is very excited by your choice of helmet.'

'Why?'

'They think that when you race, yeah, it looks like you've got a bucket on your head?'

'So what's my racing name?'

'Bucket Head. You'll like the media crew. They're funny, yeah?'

Assembly had ended with everyone clapping for Davidde. He was delighted. After he had spoken to the TV man, as he made his way around the school, he felt like a hero.

Then he got to Art.

Before they even got there, he'd suggested something to Dwayne that had never crossed his mind before.

'Hey, Dwayne, shall we go on the mitch? I want to go up the mountain and do some practice.'

The idea of skipping lessons was new to him, because before, lessons had been where he felt safest. Now he had things to do and things to prepare for, school seemed to be getting in the way. Dwayne was happy to go bunking off with Davidde, but the years of sticking to the rules kicked in with Davidde and he went to first lesson after all.

Miss Purvis-Pughes was in her storeroom with her head on a desk weeping, and Ceri Fuss was buzzing around her with tissues and a bag of make-up.

'I can't believe you made Miss cry,' she said to Davidde, as she threw a bunch of tissues into the bin, tissues stained with Miss's tears, snot and cubic inches of white foundation.

'Davidde, Davidde, is that you? Enter, enter, please come in,' she said theatrically.

When Davidde saw her, he gasped. He'd never seen her without a full mask of make-up before.

He'd always assumed that the deathly pale pallor of her face was the colour of her skin, but it wasn't. Her mascara and eyeliner had spread making her look like a panda, and Davidde half expected her to produce some bamboo shoots from under her desk, and start chewing on them as if she was in some educational zoo.

As she spoke, Ceri dabbed away at her face, assuring her that she was going to be fine, that they had the cosmetic technology to put her back together.

'Where did I go so wrong? Where, Davidde? You were the best, and now we've got less than three weeks to finish your project, and what have you done?'

Davidde said nothing because he felt so ashamed. He knew he'd done nothing.

'Do you want to be taken out of the exam? I can just concentrate on Kaitlinn then. She's almost finished her work.'

'No,' he said, 'I'll sort something out. I will.'

But he didn't sort anything out that week because he was too excited about the races.

8

That Thursday Ralph drove Davidde and Dwayne to the first race, in Abercwmffrwmpan. He'd borrowed a trailer from work and hooked it to the back of the car. Davidde was feeling confident and couldn't wait. He'd spent a lot of time with his father talking about racing and visualising things that could happen. He'd tried things out down the Rec, with Dwayne timing him and suggesting ways of improving his technique. He was ready.

When they arrived they were ushered to the technical area where they could work on the bike. The rules were that competitors weren't allowed to talk to each other and their identities had to remain a secret. Any time the competitors were seen together, either to race or have official photos taken, they had to wear their specially darkened visors and not speak. They could only reveal their faces after they had been eliminated from the competition. Two would go out tonight, two on Monday, and the final between the last two racers would be next Thursday.

Davidde, or Bucket Head as he now was, had been given a new set of blue shiny leathers but was required to wear his oversized black helmet, which had had the silhouette of a silver bucket sprayed onto the sides. Representing the village of Shwt was Mysterion, who wore black leathers, and a black helmet with a red question mark sprayed on the sides. The Glynwinci riders were Coco, who had a clown stencil on the helmet, and Tinmouth who was clad in silver. Representing Abercwmffrwmpan, the home racers and favourites, were The Zebra, decked out in black and white stripes, and Ratboy, wearing dirt-grey overalls with a helmet with pointy ears stuck on it.

As the race approached, Davidde expected to feel tense, but he didn't. He felt that maybe he should feel some nerves, but he didn't. All he had to do tonight was finish fourth or above, so statistically he had a two in three chance of going through to the next round. He didn't even have to win.

He waved when he was introduced and noticed how the hands of some of the other racers shook as they waved. He reckoned they would be nervous and make mistakes. If he couldn't get to the front, he could just wait for them to do something stupid and pass them as they slipped up. He'd been given a poor draw on the outside for the first corner so he would have to bide his time.

The riders were waiting for the gate to go down. There was a countdown from three and they were off!

Bucket Head didn't get off to a great start, but he didn't panic. He didn't want to risk getting caught in a pile-up on the first corner so he allowed everyone else to go through first. At the end of the first of three laps he was still at the back but he was in touch.

On the second lap, he began to realise that the riders here were of a much higher standard than what he was used to. He started taking a few risks but found that rather than catching up, he was still only staying in touch. By the end of the second lap he was again at the back, with Ratboy way out in front, Mysterion behind, Coco next, with Tinmouth and The Zebra going for the prized fourth spot.

Eventually Bucket Head managed to get himself half a bike-length behind The Zebra. The Zebra was doing his best to catch up with Tinmouth and on the last turn took a suicidal line and clipped the back tyre of Tinmouth and both of them span out of control. Bucket Head was aware of them falling as he raced through the gap and made it home in fourth.

He was through!

9

Davidde was tamping. He'd underestimated his opposition, and he'd only got through on luck, that was clear. Was he just expecting to turn up and walk it? He needed to up his game. He was going to practise, hard. Him and Dwayne were going to have to work much harder.

The next week they didn't bother with school. They spent days at the Rec working on strategies to make Davidde go faster. Dwayne thought that one of Davidde's problems was that he was spending too much time in the air when he went over bumps. He was rewarded for this observation by being ordered to go and find a ramp for Davidde to practise on. Dwayne thought about telling Davidde to go and find a ramp himself, but he managed to bite his tongue. He re-appeared twenty minutes later dragging an old door.

'Put it down by there,' said Davidde, 'and time me doing laps, butt.'

After another hour of practice, Davidde was happy that he was taking a much better trajectory through the air and was wasting less time.

'I'm going to do another half hour by myself, Dwayne. I don't need you. Take the door and put it in the garage to keep it safe.'

Davidde sped off and Dwayne started dragging the door towards the crooked back alley. His face was creased as he mumbled to himself, 'Who does he think he is? Does he think I'm his slave or what?'

Dwayne realised that this was the first time he'd felt hard done by since hanging round with Davidde rather than Lyndon, so he carried on dragging the door. But by the time he'd got to the alley he'd convinced himself that Lyndon and Davidde were both as bad as each other, and he threw the door in a fit of anger. It landed angled over Mr Leighton's wall. It would stay there for the rest of the week.

Ralph Nippers sat at the kitchen table. He was drinking tea. He wasn't smoking.

'And what have you got to say for yourself?'

Davidde didn't know what to say.

'I'll try again then. I had a little phone call today. From school?'

'Yeah?'

'Yeah. They say you haven't been there all week.'

'I wasn't there. I was practising.'

'So your bike is more important than school, is it?'

'When have you ever cared how I do in school?'

This was a fair point. All the years that Davidde had been a model pupil, his father hadn't paid any attention. Now he was taking days off, it seemed to matter to him. It didn't seem fair. In the past Davidde would never have challenged his father, but now he wasn't going to back down.

'Tell me. When have you ever cared?'

'Now, Davidde, I realise that over the years I may not have been the world's greatest father. And I realise that lately I may not have been here for you, and I feel a bit bad about that…

'And the thing is, I don't know about you, but I'm a man, with needs, and … what I'm trying to say is, and I don't know if you are going to like this or not, but one of the reasons I've been spending a lot of time away from the house … what I'm trying to say is I've got a girlfriend.'

Davidde didn't like it. He stood tall and looked down on his red-faced father.

'What's her name?'

'Mary. Mary Trunk. Her daughter Kaitlinn's in your class.'

10

Davidde was properly nervous for the second race at Glynwinci. Ralph drove him, though they weren't speaking, and Dwayne sat in the back of the car, awkward, saying nothing. They set the bike up in silence while Davidde thought about his opposition. They were all good, and the ones who had gone out had been good as well. He had been lucky. He'd been surprised as well because it turned out that Tinmouth had been a girl. She was named after a famous female motorcyclist she admired, not because she had a mouth made of tin. She spoke eloquently after the race and wished everybody luck for the next round. Davidde wasn't sure he would be able to be so magnanimous.

Ralph tapped him on the helmet. 'Ready to go?'

'Aye.'

Dwayne went to tap his helmet as well but Davidde moved and he ended up poking Davidde in the eye.

'Sorry, butt.'

Davidde put his visor down and drove to the starting gate. His eye was still streaming when he waved to the crowd in response to being introduced, and his hand was shaking. He just wanted to start now and get everything out of the way. He'd drawn a good starting position this time, second out from the first turn. He had to really pay attention because he still couldn't see properly out of his poked eye. When the countdown started, he was focused, and when the gate came down he went straight to the front and stayed there for the rest of the race, not seeing what went on behind him. As it turned out it was a hotly contested race with Mysterion just pipping Ratboy and Coco.

He tried to work out what it all meant. In the first race he had for most of it been last, and in the second race he had for most of it been first. A while ago all he cared about was being good in school, and now he didn't care at all. He hadn't cared about motorbikes before, now it was all he could think about. There didn't seem to be any middle ground. Was there something wrong with him?

11

On Wednesday night, the night before the final race, Davidde still hadn't spoken to his father since he'd told him he'd been going out with Kaitlinn's mother. He was seething. It seemed like a desertion. He never noticed the little kids in school looking up at him like he was a god, staring at him with their eyes wide open, wanting him to acknowledge them. He never noticed the teachers looking at him in bewilderment, wondering how someone so amenable and diligent could go off the rails so spectacularly. And he never noticed the boys his own age, some of whom admired him for becoming so cool, the others who couldn't stand him for exactly the same reason.

One thing he had noticed was that Dwayne was staying out of his way. He didn't stay with him for hours, timing laps and making suggestions. Davidde figured he'd outgrown him. There was nothing more for Dwayne to teach him. So be it, he thought, that is how it should be. The pupil leaves the teacher behind. It was like that in ancient Greece, it's like that in Maesunig now.

And the worst thing? The worst thing was the idea that at the minute, he was technically halfway to becoming Kaitlinn Trunk's stepbrother. It was an outrage. He would have to do whatever it took to jeopardise his father's relationship. He was pretty sure Kaitlinn would be feeling exactly the same. Maybe they could find some way of co-operating and stopping their parents staying together. It was, after all, in both their interests.

It was the evening before the final race. Davidde thought about his problems as he made his way back home after his final practice session down the Rec, and he saw a remarkable thing.

It was getting dark, and there was no one about.

Davidde stopped. He couldn't believe it.

Propped against the wall in his alley was a scrambler he recognised.

Mysterion's scrambler. The bike he would be racing tomorrow.

He looked around. He wondered if he could nobble it, the same way Dwayne had nobbled Lyndon's.

He could pierce the tyre. He could give it a slow puncture that hopefully wouldn't be noticed before the race. It would deflate as the race progressed, giving Davidde a much better chance of winning. It wasn't cheating, he was just optimising his chances of victory. In his pocket he had his penknife, the one Dwayne had given him with the bike. 'You never know when it'll come in handy,' he'd said. It would come in handy right now. He got it out and looked around. He opened the blade that was supposed to be for getting stones out of horses' hooves. It was the first time he'd ever needed it.

He looked around again – no one about. He got down on one knee and put the blade to tyre. He got ready to push the blade in slowly. One last look around.

He pushed the blade and the tyre resisted. It would take a real thrust to put it through the rubber. He looked around again. It would just be a tiny prick, that's all, nothing to write home about.

Then, just as he was about to plunge the point in, he sensed he was being watched. He looked over his shoulder. It was the Black Rider, head shaking in what Davidde knew was disappointment. The Black Rider turned around and walked away, head shaking all the while. Davidde's body went from tense to slack. He knew he was doing the wrong thing.

A door opening, the door to his house, a black helmet with a red question mark, a voice Davidde recognised.

'Oi, what do you think you're doing?'

Davidde stood up too quickly and the blood drained from his head. He tried to move away from the bike and protest his innocence at the same time but finished by falling over the curb, with Mysterion standing over him.

'I, I wasn't doing nothing, I was just looking at the bike.'

Mysterion took off the helmet.

Davidde was astonished.

Mysterion was Kaitlinn Trunk.

'You were going to interfere with my bike, the same way you got Dwayne to interfere with Lyndon's. I know all about you, loser.'

Davidde didn't bother denying anything.

'You're a loser, like your father. I can't see what Mam sees in him, honest to god I can't. That's what I've just been telling them.'

'Shurrup about my dad, will you? There was nothing wrong with him till he started seeing your mam. I can't cope now he's gone all sensitive.'

'Listen, loser, you're going to lose to me tomorrow like you lose to me at everything. With you it's all or nothing – be good in school, or be good at Motocross. For you it's either one or the other. Why can't you see that you can do both? You can do well in lessons, and do things outside school and be good at them, too. Boys are so stupid.'

Davidde thought about it. He had done a lot of work on his bike, and it had been to the detriment of other things. Like his Art project.

'Oh yeah, Miss Purvis-Pughes isn't very happy with you either. The Art moderators are coming the day after tomorrow to look at our projects. Mine's done. Yours isn't. You've got a day to get it done. Loser.'

That night Davidde dreamed about the Black Rider for the last time. He'd had a miserable night by himself. His father had gone with Kaitlinn's mother who was upset after they'd argued with Kaitlinn, so Ralph wasn't there to wake Davidde on the morning of the final.

He'd slept fitfully. He kept seeing the Black Rider looking on as he tried tampering with Kaitlinn's bike. Davidde would run after the Rider, but he could never catch up. He'd get close but then he would wake up covered in sweat. Finally after having the same dream four or five times, he did catch up. The Black Rider turned around and faced Davidde. The visor opened by itself. Davidde felt he should look away, he felt scared. He looked inside the helmet.

There was nothing there.

It was completely empty.

Davidde sat up in bed. It was time to get up.

His father arrived while he was having breakfast. Davidde didn't say anything to him.

He sat down opposite Davidde with a glass of juice. He looked shell-shocked.

'That Kaitlinn's a bit of a handful, isn't she?'

Davidde couldn't help but nod in agreement.

'Glad I wasn't in school with her. She's off her head, mun.'

Davidde was smiling now. It was the closest he'd felt to his father in a long time. And it was Kaitlinn who had brought them together. However, Davidde couldn't help but admire the way she'd combined her studies with her dirt-bike career. It wasn't something he'd considered possible, but she had done it. It was a great achievement.

'Now, Davidde, there's a few things I need to explain to you, before I go to work. I'll see you before the race tonight but you probably won't be in a position to listen, so it's best I talk to you now, man to man.'

He coughed.

'The thing is Davidde, despite the best efforts of Kaitlinn, Mary and me have got engaged. I know you might be a bit upset, but things move on. I'm sure your mam would have been alright with it. And we're having a party tonight, up the Club, after the race. It would be great if you could come along after your presentation.'

Davidde thought.

'I'll be there,' he said. 'Did you know Kaitlinn was Mysterion?'

'It was news to me, boy. It was news to her mother as well. She didn't know the first thing about it. She did it all when she visited her father on weekends. He's into his bikes as well, by the sound of it.'

Ralph paused for a second.

'Thanks, Dai. I'll keep a few sandwiches back for you. And there's something else I need you to do?'

'What?'

'It doesn't matter to me if you win or lose tonight. I'll still love you, you know that. But,' he paused, 'it would be great if you pulverised Kaitlinn tonight. She's been cooking my swede.'

'Don't worry, Dad,' said Davidde. 'I'll send her for fags.'

School passed in a haze. Davidde was focused on that night's race. He didn't really notice the goodwill there was towards him. Although no one was meant to know his identity, it was an open secret. Pupils and teachers wished him all the best, but he just wandered around aimlessly from lesson to lesson apart from Art which he didn't go to. He stayed in the toilets instead. He knew he had to get his art project finished by tomorrow, but he didn't know how that could be done.

Dwayne came in halfway through the lesson.

'Alright, Dwayne?'

'Alright, butt?' Dwayne didn't feel like talking.

'Any suggestions for tonight, Dwayne?'

'Not really, butt. That Mysterion looks quite good like.'

'Mysterion is Kaitlinn Trunk.'

'Shut up!'

'Serious, butt.'

Dwayne thought for a while.

'She's not used to being in the lead, so let her set the pace and stay with her for the first two laps. Don't go past her. Just wait until the final bend and open up the throttle – don't go past her before that. Her bike is probably quicker than yours over the course of the race but yours is probably quicker over a short distance. Don't leave her get too much of a lead though cos she's quite good. I mean good. And not just good for a girl either. I mean good like. I'm not trying to be sexy.'

'Sexist, Dwayne, you're not trying to be sexist.'

'Righto butt, whatever.'

Davidde put his hand on Dwayne's shoulder.

'Thanks, Dwayne.'

'No worries, butt. Stick to the game plan, OK?'

'OK.'

'Ta.'

12

That Thursday night was like a carnival in Maesunig. The sun was out and there were crowds of people milling around on the Rec waiting for the race to start, waving at the cameras and eating hot dogs and burgers from the vans that had turned up for the event. Nathaniel Grimes had come to speak to Davidde for the last time.

'Break a leg, yeah?'

'Yeah?'

'Yeah – it'll be great for ratings. Only joking. Good luck, yeah?'

'Yeah.'

For once Davidde had found a halfway house between feeling nervous and feeling confident. He was also still trying to work out how he was going to finish his Art work by tomorrow – it was a new experience to be thinking about two things at the same time.

Kaitlinn and he shook hands at the starting gate after they were introduced to the crowd, and the people cheered. Then the gate went down and they were off.

Bucket Head started well and got to the first turn before Mysterion but she was all over him. Bucket Head took a wide line on the second bend and Mysterion nipped in and was in front. For the rest of the lap Bucket Head tracked her, staying within distance of her but not trying anything risky. He thought about what Dwayne had said – don't go past her until the final turn. When it came to racing, Dwayne had always been right. Bucket Head stuck to the game plan.

Dwayne seemed to be right. On the second lap Mysterion was slower, and Bucket Head found it hard to resist passing her, but he did. On the third lap she was slower again, but Bucket Head tucked in behind her. She slowed as the lap progressed until she was at walking pace, and then finally stopped still on the final corner. Bucket Head stopped alongside her. She opened her visor.

'What are you doing?' she said.

'I'm sticking to the game plan,' said Davidde after opening his visor.

'Which is?'

'Stay with you till the last corner and pass you on the final straight.'

'And whose plan was that?'

'Dwayne's.'

'If Dwayne told you to hammer rusty nails into your eyes, would you do that?'

'Yes, if it would help me win.'

'I gave you loads of chances to pass me, and you didn't take them. If I'm honest I'm not that bothered about winning. It's just a stupid bike and I've already got one and I could do without the fuss. You should have passed me, you'd have won, but you had to stick to your game plan.'

The crowd were confused – why had they stopped? The cheering turned to silence, and then there were some boos.

Davidde thought. He said, 'You're right. Whether it's school, or bikes I concentrate on one thing and I neglect everything else. I mean, if I win this race, what do I gain?'

'A nice new bike?'

'But where's that going to get me?'

'Loads of places – it's a bike, like.'

'No, I mean deep inside me.'

'You're talking about a bike that takes you somewhere deep inside you? Are you on drugs or what?'

'Look, I haven't got time to explain, but even if I win, I want you to have it.'

'But there's a ceremony. They'll give it to the winner.'

'Tell them we can share it. I'm not going to be there. I've got to get back to school before it shuts – there's night classes on and hopefully the Art room will still be open.'

'You sure?'

'Yeah.'

'Yeah?'

'Yeah.'

'OK then. Ready, steady, go!'

Kaitlinn took off before she finished 'Go!' and her bike sped off. Davidde started after her. It was the two of them racing for the line. The crowd erupted. Davidde could feel himself smiling, could feel the bike beneath him, carrying him forward. He was gaining on Kaitlinn. They were neck and neck and stayed like that for seconds.

Eventually the speed of Davidde's bike over short distances took him past her and he crossed the finish half a wheel-length in front.

Davidde had won!

At the finish line the organisers had a garland and a bottle of pop ready to give to him on the podium, but he never stopped – he just kept riding on at full speed.

He still didn't know what to do. He was planning on going home first, picking up a few things that he could use and then going to the school. He was home before he knew it, and rode up the alley behind the house, not worrying about Mr Leighton seeing him. It was too late for worrying about stuff like that now. He roared on up the alley, but there was an obstacle in his way – the door Dwayne had discarded, angled like a ramp over Mr Leighton's wall.

13

Mr Leighton had been tending to his tomatoes in his greenhouse. Mrs Leighton was fond of saying that he loved his tomatoes more than he loved his wife, and in a way she was right. The tomatoes never nagged him or rolled their eyes when he said something they disagreed with. He tended to them with a great tenderness, and they grew and he ate them. And this was going to be a bumper crop, and they'd be ready in a week or so. Mr Leighton was pleased with his work, slid the door shut on his greenhouse and retired to the patio for a mug of tea in the evening sun.

He reflected that he had been a bit grumpy lately, but now the sun was out, his greenhouse was tidy and his tomatoes were thriving, everything was fine. Not even the sound of one of those scramblers in the distance could affect his mood. He'd stopped phoning the police about scramblers now as well. It was a battle that he was never going to win, so as long as they kept to their patch of land he wouldn't bother the local constabulary. He was aware that there had been a competition that night. Well, as long as they weren't coming here, he wasn't going to worry about it.

The sound of the bike seemed to be coming closer. Mr Leighton did his best not to react to it, but he was little bit annoyed now. It got louder still. Confused, he stood up. He needed to go out the alley and see what was happening. Louder still, then the sound of the bike colliding with something. He saw at eye level a helmet appearing over his back wall. Then arms, a body and handlebars, and the whole bike travelling in a perfect parabola over his wall. For a second at the very peak of its arc, the bike and rider seem to hang perfectly still in the sky, and even Mr Leighton was aware of the sheer beauty of what he was seeing. Then he realised there was nothing he could do to stop it going through his greenhouse.

The front wheel pierced the roof; there was a

sound of cracking and then glass smashing on the floor. The bike lurched through the glass and Davidde followed it through, the suspension cushioning him from the blow when the bike hit the ground. He got thrown over the handlebars of his mangled bike and he landed flat on his back in his leathers at Mr Leighton's feet.

There was a moment of stillness. Davidde opened his eyes. There were clouds in the sky. He felt confident that he wasn't dead. His leathers had protected him and he'd been thrown clear of most of the glass. He was glad about this. There was a human shape standing over him. He sat up slowly. He could still move.

He pulled off his helmet.

'You!' cried Mr Leighton, as he reached out for one of his battered tomato plants and started hitting Davidde over the head with it.

'Let him carry on,' thought Davidde to himself stoically. 'I deserve this. Let him do his worst.'

Mrs Leighton came out to see what the commotion was. She was so surprised to see her husband attacking her teenage neighbour with his plants among the debris of glass and scrambler that at first she couldn't say a word. But she felt she had to step in when Mr Leighton started throwing fat, ripe tomatoes at Davidde's head as hard as he could at point-blank range.

'What on earth is going on?'

'Mrs Leighton, Mr Leighton. You've been really good to me and Dad over the years. You've helped bring me up, helped me with the things Dad couldn't help with. I thank you for that. And lately, well, I know I haven't been around much, but I made a few choices, some of them wrong. But I've been on a journey, see, and the last part of the journey didn't go very well, what with me driving my bike through your greenhouse. But I can fix the greenhouse, I promise, I've just run into some money. The thing is, I know this is the wrong time to ask, but I really need a favour. I need to take a few things to school in your car.'

14

The next morning Miss Pughes-Pervis drove to school with a ferocity Mr Rastud had never experienced before. He pretended to be asleep while she tore up the narrow streets. She was angry that she'd been let down by Davidde. She thought about all the help she'd given him over the years, and all the lies he'd told her recently. She was going to look like a fool in front of the moderators. She was going to have to get another job. She couldn't cope with being let down so badly.

In her room Kaitlinn's work took up one corner, her three-dimensional Celtic Horse, all lively colours and bright ideas, executed with skill and precision. But the middle of the room had changed. The tables had been moved out, and there was a bike with its front wheel and handlebars flat against the floor and its rear wheel in the air, as if it had just come through the ceiling. Around it was glass, a greenhouse, with a hole in the top where it looked like the bike had come through. Bits of glass were hanging from strings. It was the recreation of the moment just after a scrambler had gone through the roof of a greenhouse.

Davidde had done an installation! He'd used the title The Joy of Wrecks!

Miss Pughes-Pervis' spirits lifted. It was a good piece of work, not as good as Kaitlinn's, but good enough to pass. Somehow Davidde hadn't let her down.

The previous night, after finishing his work at school with the help of Mr and Mrs Leighton, Davidde had made it to the engagement party, which was still in full swing at 10 o'clock.

He received a hero's welcome, shaking hands with people and even, to his surprise, getting on quite well with Kaitlinn. Mr Leighton and Mrs Leighton came along too, and Dwayne and the boys were there as well.

It was warm and sticky in the club, especially for Davidde who still had bits of tomato in his hair. He went outside to get a little air.

On the way he bumped into Dwayne.

'Where you been, butt?' he said.

'I just finished my Art project.'

'No way! Miss will be landed.'

'Dwayne, I want to say thanks. You've been a real good friend to me.'

They shook hands.

'Look, I gorra go,' said Dwayne. 'I need to give these pork scratchings to Ceri.'

'You do that, Dwayne. She'll enjoy them.'

Davidde went outside.

As he stood on the pavement, there was the sound of a bike. It came up the street and stopped directly in front of Davidde. It was the Black Rider.

The visor raised again. This time a face was visible. The Black Rider smiled with pride at Davidde, then shut the visor and rode off, disappearing into thin air, for the last time.

15

The Black Rider was Davidde's mam.

About the Author

Huw Davies grew up in Nantyffyllon, near Maesteg and studied English before becoming an English teacher. He always wanted to be a writer, but it took him a while to realise that in order to achieve this he would actually need to do some writing.

As a teacher, he came to feel that there was a lack of what he called 'daft books for boys', and started work on *Scrambled*. The book is set in the fictional town of Maesunig, which is loosely based on Maesteg, Nantyffyllon and Cymer in South Wales.

Huw is also a member of the bilingual Gonzo Power Pop outfit Nimrodsound, a unit so successful that they once supported a band who had a song used on an advertisement on TV (he thinks it was for a car but it could have been for slug pellets). He lives in Carmarthen with his wife and three children, where he has embraced middle age by taking up running. *Scrambled* is his first book for children.